Book Reviews

"Raleigh Minard's 'Phoenix Reborn' is an epic tale of one man's struggle to reclaim his lost kingdom and free his people from the tyranny of the guild masters. Phoenix is a brave and determined hero who faces many challenges, including the deadly Bettle Men from another world. He ultimately succeeds in conquering another land and building a worldwide Kingdom.

Minard is a skilled storyteller, and 'Phoenix Reborn' is a well-written and engaging book. It is clear that he has a deep understanding of human nature and the dynamics of power. This is a book that will appeal to fans of historical fiction and fantasy alike."

—**Reprospace Editorial Reviews™**

Phoenix Reborn

PHOENIX REBORN
First edition, published 2022

By Raleigh Minard

Cover design by Reprospace.com

Paperback ISBN-13: 978-1-95-268550-7

Published by Kitsap Publishing
Poulsbo, WA 98370
www.KitsapPublishing.com

Acknoledgments

To my LORD who provide inspirations
and imagination.

Thank You!

Prolog

This is a brief history of the Phoenix the King. Randal was our creator and leader. Randal created a machine that combined humans with animals. This gave us a new life and allowed us to change back and forth from human to animal or something in between. Randal moved us to a small island where we could live our lives. Over time our animal side began to dominate our human side, and we broke up into factions, and wars broke out. We were fighting for space, food, and water. Somehow the US Navy found out we were there on the island and sent in troops to destroy us when a man named Paladin showed up and brought us to this new planet through a portal.

Randal tried to govern us via the constitutional way of America, but we resorted to a feudal system of governing overtime. At the end of Randal's life, Randal was gibbering away about some prophecy of a Phoenix who'll conquer the world. Many centuries passed, and the prophecy was forgotten. One group of people were Avarians (or bird people) who moved off to the wilderness to be by themselves and bread true to themselves only. Over time the inbreeding created the boy who will become the Phoenix.

The boy would be born to Todd and Pam through an arranged marriage; Pam was typical for a wife of the Chimerians she kept the house and the garden; she would hunt in her eagle form and supply meat for the table. Todd, the father, was a tradesman and was off selling a small herd of sheep-like animals on the coast. When Todd was deep in his cups one night, Todd was bragging about the money he was making from the sale. When two men who were staying at the inn heard him. That night they decided to relieve Todd of his money. When the men find out that Todd has no money, they killed him.

Pam was great with the child back at home, and her mother-in-law and her mother helped her with the birth. It was a boy, but he was born a eunuch. The mother-in-law wanted to take the boy into the woods and leave him for the scavengers to kill; Pam wouldn't hear of it, and neither would her mother. The boy grew up with his mother and her parents. When the boy could swing a hammer, grandfather brought him into the smithy and taught him how to work with metal.

The boy grew up, and as his name day approached, the boy did a remarkable thing he was able to change for the first time into a bird. He liked the falcon because of the speed, so he became one and flew out to the mountain where his grandfather had found the star sone he liked to work with. The boy landed on the mountain because he thought he saw a shiny rock and was curious. As the boy lands, a solar flare hits him full-on, burning up his clothes and rendering him unconscious. His grandfather was out for his morning flight, grandfather spots the burst of light and goes to investigate. Zeke finds the boy lying on the ground with all his clothes burned off and not a mark on the boy. Zeke wakes the boy to ask what happened to him. The boy couldn't tell his grandfather. All he could remember was a flash of light. "Let's return to the smithy and get you some of my old clothes," says Zeke.

The boy changes into a phoenix bird glowing hot and brilliant, causing grandfather to back away and yell at the boy to change back into a boy, with some instruction from Zeke. Zeke got the boy to change into a falcon, and they flew back to the smithy. Over time the boy became the Phoenix in name and form and conquered his kingdom. Over time Phoenix proved the prophecy true, and he'll test the final part by dying in a fire to be reborn.

Phoenix grew old, grey-haired, and worn-looking, but he still had vitality and strength. During the last four hundred years of Phoenix's life, when he wasn't protecting the kingdom from the sea raiders, he would take down rulers and set up new ones when that ruler wouldn't follow Phoenix's mandates. Phoenix made many enemies from within and without the kingdom. The vultures were waiting for the King to die so that someone among their number could rise up and take charge.

Phoenix spent most of his time at Zeke's cottage because of the smithy. He let his place in the valley go. It was too painful for him to visit there. Then one night, Phoenix came to my son Raymond and me to carry us from castle Phoenix to Zeke's cottage to be witnesses to his final act. He was to fly to the mountain to die. His funeral pyre was ready. One of two things could happen: he'd be reborn as in the legends, or he'd die and be with Alana, his dead wife.

"Hector, my old friend, and your son Raymond I'm going to that mountain (Points Phoenix); you should be able to see the fire from here. Wait three days. Make sure you give me three days. If I don't return, you may go live your lives. If the legend is correct, I'll be back."

"Good luck, Sire."

Phoenix flies up to the mountain and lands on his funeral pyre. Phoenix using his power sets his funeral pyre on fire with his last bit of strength. As he burns up with the wood. Phoenix lies there, watching the flame consume the wood. As he watched, he wondered if he would feel the burning. Soon he falls into a bottomless void of darkness as everything turned to ash. Hector and Raymond can see the fire on the mountain. They whisper their goodbyes to their King. The scribes return to the cottage and settle in to write what just happened in the book of history. With hope, the legend is correct, knowing that the wars that will start if the legend is not true. It will destroy all the kingdoms with wars.

Hector waited, and each morning he'd watch the mountain hoping to see the Phoenix return. On the third day, both Hector and Raymond watch the mountain. They are hoping against hope that the Phoenix will appear. They grow tired of watching, and just as they turn to gather their gear for the return trip home, Raymond sees a flash of brilliant light.

Phoenix, for three days, floats in a void of darkness, then on the third day, Phoenix experiences a great flash of light and extreme heat as he explodes from the ashes of his pyre.

"Father, see that?!"

"See what, Raymond?"

"That father!" as Raymond points at the light coming their way, "it's the Phoenix!"

The Phoenix flies from the mountain toward Zeke's cottage and lands with a thunderous cry. Phoenix lands in the yard. He is looking regal in his new golden body with fire shimmering about his body. At first, Phoenix doesn't know the scribe, Hector; then Phoenix changes into his human form. Phoenix looks not to be much older than Raymond.

"I remember you, Hector, I remember," says Phoenix.

"Sire, you need to reappear at all the castles and towns before war can erupt," warns Hector.

Phoenix takes heed of Hector's warning and makes ready to set off to prove he is still their King.

I lay down my pen, the Phoenix's next thousand-year reign begins, and my son Raymond will record it during his time here. This is where my writing ends, and Raymond's begins.

"I Raymond, pick up where my father left off recording the acts of my King the Phoenix. I'll pass off my duty to a successor for the next three hundred years. Now I'll set pen to paper as I follow my King and tell of his exploits that I've seen or that he has related to me."

CHAPTER

1

Well, Raymond and Hector, are you ready to return to Castle Phoenix?"

"Yes, Sire, we need to make haste before war breaks out; as I said, you need to reappear to those in power so they'll not rise and usurp the kingdom."

Phoenix changes into his giant form of a Phoenix, scoops up both men and flies back to the castle to announce his return. Phoenix reaches the castle in the late evening when the shadows grow long from the setting sun. As he hovers above the castle, he screams out like thunder and sheds light like the sun as he settles into the courtyard and releases the scribes.

Everyone pours out of their homes and the castle to see the commotion and realize that the Phoenix did not die of old age. Most people are overjoyed, while the nobles harbor hate their King, who is for the people instead of the nobility.

In the past, the nobility was in charge, and even after three generations, the nobles still harbored ill will towards their King, who stripped them of their so-called wealth (Slavery). The nobles were chomping at the bit to be rulers over the people—all the land in the region. The nobles forget that their ancestors were much poorer than the nobles of today.

It's the power and obeisance they want. Now with Phoenix back, they can't have it. Jacob is the great-great-grandson of Mary, the queen regent. Jacob is now the regent of Castle Phoenix. Jacob, most of all, hates Phoenix for killing his great, great ancestor King Phoenix and taking his rulership. Jacob now fawns over Phoenix in hopes of deceiving Phoenix that he's a loyal subject and his friend.

Phoenix re-establishes his rule at Castle Phoenix and prepares to head to the main meeting center built during the time of Queen Mary, where Phoenix will communicate to all other kingdoms to let them know he's still in charge.

The night that Phoenix returned, Jacob was beside himself with hatred, needing to get away from the castle and the presents of Phoenix. After the evening meal, Jacob stole away from the castle in his black panther form. Jacob ranged out into the edge of the forest, where he found a herd of sheep-like animals. Jacob stalks the herd and selects one to kill. With stealth, Jacob stalks the animal and, on silent feet, edges up close to the animal in the dark; then, with a roar, Jacob pounces upon one of the animals and tears its throat out, and feeds on the parts he likes best.

Jacob finishes his grisly meal when a raven flies out of a nearby tree to land on the animal and starts pecking at the leftovers of the kill. Jacob roars at the raven and makes ready to strike when the bird changes into an elderly man. "Jacob?" He asks. Jacob stops in his tracks and changes to his human form. "Who wants to know?" Jacob states.

"I'm called Devlin, your majesty."

"I'm not king here, just a regent," complains Jacob.

"My mistake, sir, I'm an old wonderer looking for and finding knowledge; I have been a teacher in my time."

Laughing, Jacob asks, "teaching what, Devlin?"

"Many things, young Jacob."

"Like what?" asks Jacob.

"Math, Science, Alchemy, History, and such," says Devlin.

"What could you teach me then, Devlin?" mocks Jacob.

Devlin takes a long look at Jacob as if he asses his following words. "Let's say, Jacob, that we both have a similar goal to bring down Phoenix for our own reasons. I could teach you how to do that," suggests Devlin.

Jacob looks at Devlin with distrust in his eyes, trying to decide if he should trust this person or is he a spy for the King, testing his loyalty.

"Why should I trust you, Devlin? You could be with the kings' men checking my loyalty."

Devlin looks at Jacob then it is as if he decides; Devlin opens his shirt to show Jacob his brand that the Phoenix had branded on his chest years ago.

"Jacob, do you know what this brand means?" queries Devlin.

"I've seen it before, but I never understood it."

"It's death to the one who wears it. If a king's man finds me here in this country, I would be killed," explains Devlin.

"I see," answered Jacob.

Devlin spoke, "you see, Jacob, I was once the head of the guild masters from across the eastern sea; I was trying to usurp the Phoenix many years ago and lost."

"I believe you, Devlin, maybe we can help each other, now that we have something worthy of death against each other. Me for treason, and you for your brand."

"Quite so, Jacob. My camp is just beyond the trees over there, let's go collect my things, and we can go to the castle."

Devlin leads the way to his camp, where he collects his few meager things, and they head for the castle. An hour later, Jacob enters the castle with Devlin and engages a steward to find Devlin a room and provide him with some food and drink. In the morning, Jacob introduces Devlin to Phoenix and tells Phoenix that Devlin is a teacher, and Jacob wants permission to engage Devlin in that capacity.

Phoenix is always ready to have people learn new things and gives his permission. Phoenix turns to Devlin to ask what he would be teaching Jacob when he is struck with a thought that he has met this Devlin before, sometime in the past. Then Phoenix brushes it aside and welcomes Devlin.

CHAPTER

2

Jacob, I must take my leave of you and travel to other holds and visit them. You take care and learn your studies. I'll see you when I return," pronounces Phoenix.

Both Jacob and Devlin bow to Phoenix and follow him out into the courtyard, where they watch him change into the Phoenix bird form and watch as he flies off toward the west.

"Now, young Jacob, we shall learn all we can about our King, and in getting that knowledge, we may discover his weakness," speaks Devlin.

"Let us go to the library, Devlin, to see what has been written about him," suggests Jacob.

"You are learning, Jacob."

The two retire to the library to locate and read everything about The Phoenix they can find. Phoenix travels for several months visiting the other parts of his kingdom to see how they fare. He had to take down a leader or two in a few places and replace them with someone else, creating more enemies. At one hold, Phoenix encounters a man whose father he knew very well, and Phoenix stops by to visit only to learn that the man died some time ago.

Phoenix pays his regrets to the young man when Phoenix sees a knife in the man's belt.

"Castor, may I see your knife?" queries Phoenix.

"Sure," as Castor hands the knife over to Phoenix.

Phoenix looks the knife over and asks where Castor got it. Castor replies, "I purchased it from a merchant about two months ago. Why do you ask Sire?"

"Castor, I was the one to forge the knife from star stone as a gift to Angus, who managed the Southern kingdom. Then the knife was handed down to his son and then to his son. I wonder how it got clear up here?"

"As I recall, the merchant said that the man who sold it to him needed money. When I saw it, I made an offer to the merchant, and he jumped on the price I offered," explained Castor.

"What did you offer the merchant for it, if I may ask?"

"I gave him two gold coins," said Castor.

"He must not have known what it was made of, or he'd have held out for ten times that amount," stated Phoenix.

Like most people with a knife, we must test it to see if it cuts, and Phoenix accidentally slices his hand, and the blood oozes out as a fiery liquid that sets fire to the wooden floor of Castor's house. Phoenix steps on it to put out the fire. Phoenix takes a vile (of his tears) from his pocket and pours the liquid on the wound, and the bleeding stops, but the wound doesn't heal up.

"Castor, I'm sorry about your floor; I didn't know my blood would do that."

"No problem sire, a little sanding and polishing will fix it right up, but let me get a bandage for your hand."

"Thank you! Castor."

Castor returns with a bandage and a pot full of salve. Castor slathers the salve onto Phoenix's hand and covers it with a bandage. "Will you be ok, sire?"

"I think so, Castor, I've never cut myself with a star stone before, so I wasn't prepared for what happened."

"Sire, don't tell anyone about this, or your enemies might discover this."

"Very true, Castor, Let's keep this quiet."

Phoenix returns Castor's knife, bids him a good day, and steps outside to fly off to the south to visit the poison dart people. It takes a several days to reach them in the far southern jungle, and he lands in the clearing of the village. The people come out with spears and bows drawn to attack until Phoenix identifies himself. The village elder keeps back but greets the Phoenix.

Phoenix holds out his hand for a handshake upon meeting the elder, but the elder refuses. The elder is fearful he might poison the Phoenix with his touch. Phoenix takes the elders hand and shakes it. The villagers watch to see if the Phenix will die from the poison. Then nothing happens, in their language, Phoenix explains he was given the antidote years ago by Fenwick, who had discovered it. After a brief visit with the Dart people, the Phoenix resumes his travel to his other holdings.

While the Phoenix was away, Devlin was also busy combing the library for any information on the Phoenix with Jacob's help. Then one afternoon, Devlin left Jacob in the library to go flying off into the woods to meet his underlings and pass on some of his findings to his master. Devlin lands next to the glade where the camp is set up. As he changes from a raven to himself, a guild master steps out of the tent.

"Well, Devlin, what news do you have?" asks Maxim.

"Nothing yet, Maxim; the Phoenix is still a mystery; I've learned that he's the one in the prophecy, but nothing on how to get rid of him."

"Do you have any other information about him?" queries Maxim.

"Yes, some of the regents would like to see the Phoenix gone as much as we would, especially that young idiot Jacob. We'll have to get rid of him shortly after we dispose of the Phoenix. He's too easy to lead around by the nose," chuckles Devlin.

"That's good to know; he may become useful before we kill him, so treat him well, Devlin."

"If you say so, Maxim. I'd best be getting back to the castle before that buffoon comes looking for me."

"We'll see you in a few days, Devlin; I hope you gather some good news."

"Yes, Maxim." Devlin changes into his raven form and flies off to the castle.

Devlin flies into the open door of the castle and lands in the lower gallery, where he changes back into his human form and collects some fruit off the table, and heads back to the library where Jacob is reading.

"Here, Jacob is something to eat while we work."

"Thank you, Devlin."

"Have you found anything Jacob while I was out?"

"The only thing I found was in the book of tribes; Phoenix found the lost tribe of the poison dart people."

"Does it say where they are? Jacob."

"No, just someplace in the south."

"I see," muses Devlin. "With all we have reviewed, we've not found any weakness for the Phoenix."

"That doesn't surprise me, Devlin. Would you write about any weakness you might have for all to, see?"

"Now that you mentioned it, Jacob, you may be right," muses Devlin.

"Devlin, it's getting late; we should turn in; maybe we can think about it tomorrow; Phoenix will be returning tomorrow or the next day. We may get a fresh idea with a clearer mind," complains Jacob.

"You're right, Jacob; let's turn in."

They both retire to their rooms. Devlin opens his window and waves a candle back and forth in the open window calling for the person down in the courtyard to fly up to his room.

"Devlin, my master, what do you require of me?" asks the servant.

"Come in, Stillwell; I have a message for the guild masters at the camp. The Poison Dart people are located in the south. We need to relocate them," states Devlin.

"Are you sure, master?"

"Yes, the Phoenix himself put it into the book of tribes. We've been searched for them throughout the years. The guild master who knew the location died before he could tell me where. Now we have a location to go look for them. Now go and tell the master," Commanded Devlin.

"I'll make haste and tell the guild masters at the camp what you've learned, my master."

"Yes, Stillwell, go before you're discovered."

Stillwell flies down into the courtyard and out of the gate into the darkness, and lands in the empty field before he changes into a dog (crows do not fly well in the dark) and runs off into the woods where the camp is located to relay the message from Devlin about the poison dart people.

Devlin turns back to his thoughts after Stillwell departs. "If I'm going to find a weakness, I'll need to spy on Phoenix to see if I can discover it for myself," Thinks Devlin.

Chapter

3

The next day Phoenix returns from one of his visits, and Jacob meets him at the castle entrance. Phoenix greets Jacob as he lands, "Hello Jacob, and how fairs the kingdom?"

"It's doing, as usual, well, my king, and how was your trip?"

"Surprisingly well, I've reasserted my presents with all the holdings, and everyone is doing as I have commanded. Some of them still resent my kingship, but they'll comply." Phoenix asks a question, "Where is your friend Devlin?"

"Devlin left to travel to the east and promised he'd return in a few weeks," commented Jacob.

"Too bad, I was hoping to have a conversation with him, well next time then. I need to clean up and get some food. I'm tired and gritty."

"Sire, I'll attend to the food while you bathe. Do you want it here in the hall or sent to your room?"

"I'll have it here in the hall, Jacob. Thank you!"

Phoenix left to go to his royal apartment to clean up and change. At the same time, Jacob went to the kitchen to order some food brought for the Phoenix. Earlier, Devlin made a show of leaving to continue his travels, and he promised he would return to continue Jacob's mentoring. Devlin walked a league eastward from the castle and located a place in the woods where he could hide his travel bag and walking stick.

Devlin then changed into a crow, flew back to the castle. Devlin flew in through one of the open doors, and returned to his apartment, where he transformed into a rat. Devlin then sneaks down from his apartment into the great hall and hides so he can spy on Phoenix. Devlin follows the Phoenix for several weeks and can find nothing other than what he already knew. Devlin discovers nothing that can be used against the Phoenix to get rid of him or kill him.

One afternoon Phoenix heads out of the castle and walks over to the smithy to see if he can trade with the smith for some time at the forge so he can make a star stone gift for someone. Phoenix enters the smithy and looks around at the swords hanging from the walls. He selects one, flexes it, and notices that it's brittle and would shatter if used in a sword fight. (Not far away, Devlin the rat hiding in the shadows is watching.) The smith meets up with Phoenix without realizing who he is.

"May I help you, sir?" queries Orion.

"Yes, what's your name?" asks Phoenix.

"I'm called Orion."

"Really? I heard that there was an Orion who worked here years ago. Are you related?" asks Phoenix.

"Yes, he was my great, great grandfather."

"I knew him; I had my grandfather Zeke train him in forging; how would you like me to train you?" asked Phoenix.

"How could you have known him? You're not much older than I am, sir," queries Orion.

"Would it explain how I knew him if you knew that I am the Phoenix?"

Getting down on one knee, "Sire, please forgive me. I didn't realize who you are."

Laughing, Phoenix helps Orion up. "It's alright, Orion, don't bow to me; I feel we'll become fast friends. Now here's what I propose, I'll teach you what I know, and you allow me to use your tools and forge from time to time, deal? As a bonus, I'll throw in some of the tall tales of your great, great grandfather."

"Anything you say, Sire! I'd like that."

"We're going to have to change that, don't call me sire here in your smithy, call me Todd, and it won't seem awkward to talk with me," commands Phoenix.

"Yes, Sir..., I mean Todd."

"Now, Orion, this sword would shatter with the first good blow; it needs to be tempered; let me show you how." (Devlin kept watch and learned that Phoenix's father's name is Todd, it's not much, but it may come in handy in the future.)

A day or two later Phoenix returns to his grandfather's cottage and picks up all the tools for engraving that Phoenix made for himself and returns to castle Phoenix to make a present to Orion; of the tools, for doing metal engraving, which he decides to teach young Orion to do. Phoenix takes Orion through the process of tempering the sword, and over time, Phoenix fills in the missing gaps in Orion's knowledge of forging steel. Orion's work improves, gaining him a good reputation with all the farmers.

At the same time, the sea raiders make landfall in the deep south to look for the lost tribe of the poison dart people. Devlin is spying on Phoenix and Orion the whole time, looking for the one thing that would help Devlin rid himself of the Phoenix. The watch station that Phoenix set up years ago in the south was maned to get word back to the Phoenix if the sea raiders were to show again. The two men there spotted the sea raiders, and split up. One went north to the southern castle to warn of the sea raiders, and the other man flew to the area where the lost tribe lived to warn them of the sea raiders.

The man that flew north would take a week to reach the southern castle. The man winging his way to the lost tribe would be there in a few hours. He lands at the edge of the village and stands there, showing his hands open, to prove he is no threat. The village elder meets with him, and the man warns the elder of the tribe of the sea raiders that just landed on the coast. Then he flew off to the north to make contact with the Phoenix as instructed, and it will take better of a month to travel there to castle Phoenix.

Phoenix teaches Orion to forge starstone, and he helps Orion make a knife out of the stone. After polishing the knife, Orion cuts himself on the very sharp blade. To stop the bleeding, Phoenix takes out a small vial of his tears and pours it on the wound, and it stops bleeding; in a minute more, the wound heals. It's not like Orion has never cut himself while he is working.

"Todd, what did you pour on my hand?" asks Orion.

"My tears, they heal just about anything."

CHAPTER

4

Castor shows up to see the Phoenix; as he enters the castle, Castor gets directed to the smithy where the Phoenix is.

"Ho! Sire, are you here?" calls out Castor as he enters the smithy.

"Castor! Is that you?" replies Phoenix.

"Yes, Sire, I've come to give you something and look at your hand."

Phoenix holds up his hand, and "it's all healed up. Thanks, Castor, that salve worked very well." (Devlin perks up to listen to the conversation. It may be interesting.)

Castor fishes around in his bag, pulls out a jar full of the salve that he used on Phoenix's hand, and gives it to Phoenix. "Here, Sire, you may need to use it again from the looks of this place."

"No, Castor, I'm being cautious; my last accident taught me that. Oh, Castor, this young man is my friend Orion who owns this smithy. Orion, this is my friend Castor from the west providences.

"

You two should get to know each other; I think you'll become fast friends."

"If you don't mind me asking what happened to you, Phoenix, that you needed the salve?" asked Orion.

"I cut myself with a starstone knife, and I didn't heal as fast as I usually do; in fact, my blood set Castor's floor on fire. Then Castor put the salve on my hand and bandaged it up. That stopped the bleeding." (Devlin heard every word, then crept out of the smithy using the shadows, once outside, he changed to a raven and flew to the guild master's camp deep in the woods.)

Devlin told the guild master what he had just learned about the starstone and how it could cut the Phoenix. At first, the master asked "what good will that do?"

Devlin reviled that "if you can cut him, the starstone can kill him."

"The next step will be to get a starstone knife or sword to use on the Phoenix," said the guild master.

"I have it!" shouts Devlin. "The starstone sword is hanging on the back of the throne at castle Phoenix."

"What starstone sword?" asks the guild master.

"Phoenix mounted a starstone sword up on the back of the throne a thousand years ago when he became the king. His grandfather made it for him for his name day, according to history. And to think his one weakness has been there this whole time," muses Devlin.

"Let's not get ahead of ourselves, Devlin; we still don't have the sword."

"We will master, we will. I'll return and steal it myself. I think it's time for me to return to the castle as myself and enlist that stupid regent Jacob to help me."

"Devlin, when will you have the sword?" asks the guild master.

Devlin pauses and then answers, "I can steal it in a month and return it here."

The guild master purses his lips and tapes the side of his face, "Make it two months, Devlin. I need time to set certain plans into motion. You've served me well. Now return and set things in motion on your end," commanded the head guild master.

"Yes, master." Devlin returns to where he stashed his satchel and walking stick to make it look like he's returning from his journey of exploration.

Late that day, Devlin walks up to the castle gates and enters as if from a long trip, and Jacob meets him in the great hall and asks the staff to bring food and drink for Devlin, and he sits down to regale Jacob about his adventure. (It was all a pack of lies.)

The following day Devlin enters the throne room to look at the starstone sword to see what he will need to remove it from the back of the throne. Phoenix walks in and sees Devlin looking at the sword.

"What has you so interested in the sword Devlin?" again, Phoenix has a feeling he has met Devlin in the past but can't quite place where.

"Morning, your majesty, I was admiring your sword; it's like no sword I've ever seen before," said Devlin.

"I'd be surprised if you had; it's one of a kind. My grandfather Zeke made it from starstone," says Phoenix.

Devlin thanks Phoenix and decides to leave the throne room before Phoenix realizes who Devlin is and kills him for being back in his kingdom. Devlin takes his leave of the king and goes to find Jacob to continue Jacob's instruction of history.

Phoenix watches Devlin as he walks away; somewhere in his mind, it's screaming that he knows Devlin by another name. "Why is he interested in the starstone sword?" muses Phoenix.

Phoenix remembers he has to go to Orion's forge to teach Orion more about engraving metal and gold inlay. On his way to Orion's, Phoenix ponders Devlin; there are too many warning signs about the man. Who is he? thinks Phoenix.

Phoenix puts his thoughts aside and turns to the task at hand. Devlin watches Phoenix as he walks out the castle doors; Devlin realizes Phoenix may be remembering him from the past. Then Devlin decides to avoid Phoenix until it's too late for the Phoenix. Devlin devises a way to steal the starstone sword from the throne room. Devlin makes a drawing of the star sword; then, he manages to get one of his sea raider blacksmiths smuggled into the castle to look at the sword to see if he can forge a duplicate one out of steel to be used to replace the real starstone sword. Devlin waits until Phoenix leaves to go to the west to visit one of his landowners to see how they're doing.

Devlin brought in the sea raider blacksmith so he could take measurements of the sword. With the drawing and the measurements, the smith changes into an eagle and flies off to the east coast to one of the camps of the sea raiders to fabricate the replacement sword of plain steel. So, they can steal the real starstone sword and replace it with the fake one. When the sword was forged, they made up a caravan to bring it to castle Phoenix.

The night before the Phoenix arrived, Devlin with his henchmen snuck into the throne room and replaced the starstone sword. Back in the woods, Devlin met with the guild master and finalized their plans to kill Phoenix and usurp all his kingdoms.

At the same time, down in the deep south, the raiders managed to find the poison dart people, and they tried to ambush the village. Then when they realized the village had been warned about their presents, they became the ambushed. The villages dropped from the trees to touch the intruders causing them to die from their poison touch. All but one young teenager died, and the girl who was the villager's medicine woman took pity on the young man thinking she could turn him like them, much like her grandsire Fenwick from years ago.

Mara saved the young man and gave him the antidote against the poison of her people. She hid him in her hut that night, and in the morning, he had run away and was heading back to the beach where the raiders camped. Mara ran to the elders and told them what she did, and the elder sent his best trackers and hunters to kill the boy. The tribe moved deeper into the jungle and up into the high trees. In the meantime, Mara is exiled from the tribe.

Two days later, the trackers locate the boy, and he was almost within shouting distance of the raider camp when one of the hunters shot the boy with a bow. And he dies instantly. The two men crept up on the boy and then dragged him into the jungle to leave him.

Days later, the raiders send more men to locate the village; all they find is an empty village and their dead comrades. From her hiding place, Mara watches them until they leave. Mara decides to move deeper into the jungle and make a new home. She returns to her hut and collects some of her things and travels west from where she is; as she goes, she collects many plants to make medicines, something her mother passed on to her. Mara builds a new hut in the days that follow and moves all her things from her old hut to her new hut. On one occasion, Mara encounters a raiding party looking for her people. Mara manages to evade them and keep hidden.

Phoenix returns to castle Phoenix, and it appears something is not correct. Many of his people are in the courtyard cheering him on for some reason. Usually, no one is gathered to greet him unless he announces his presents. Phoenix lands on the upper platform and changes to his human form.

Phoenix speaks out, "Why are you all here?"

Devlin steps out from the crowd, "We are gathered here to watch you die, Sire."

"Well, Rex, I see you've finally shown your colors. You also know I intend to kill you if you ever returned to my country."

Devlin (Rex) held his hand up, "Don't try anything, my lord, or all these people here will be put to death."

"How so, Rex?" queries Phoenix.

"If you will notice each person has a guard by them and each guard has a knife held to their backs, one move on your part will see them killed."

"Alright, Rex, what's your game?" commands Phoenix.

"You will fight my champion he's called the Beast; he's quite the killing machine. He'll be using your starstone sword."

"You know I can take him out with my power Rex."

"I know so; I'm asking you for your word you won't do that, or Orion and Jacob here will be killed the moment you do," says Rex.

"Do I get a weapon to use, Rex?"

"Of course, use your rapier," smirks Rex.

"I see; you want all the cards stacked in your favor, Rex," mocks Phoenix.

"Yes, Sire, today you will die, and I'll step up and rule this country," mocks Devlin.

"Ok, Rex, before you bore me to death, let's get this over with," commands Phoenix.

One of the staff brings Phoenix his rapier and under his breath, "My lord, we're ready to die for you."

Phoenix thanks the man and whispers, "not all is lost."

Phoenix gets into his dance position with his sword, also made from starstone. The Beast mounts the upper platform in his armor and swings the starstone sword. The Beast hoping to kill the Phoenix quickly brings the blade down hard, and Phoenix dances out of the way, and he probes the Beast's armor with his sword tip leaving the Beast with a couple of cuts. While the Phoenix is dancing about realizing that the starstone sword can kill him, he looks to see where all the enemy is stationed about him.

Most of the men have crossbows, so he won't be able to take them all out. Phoenix forgets one rule of the Dance master's directions. "When fighting for your life, don't follow the rules." Phoenix gets preoccupied, and the Beast lands a cut deep into Phoenix's side. Phoenix realizes he'll die if he is struck again. Then he realizes what he'll have to do. Blood is setting fire to the stone patio as he bleeds. Phoenix realizes he has to die. Phoenix transforms into the Phoenix, then launches into the air then creates an explosion in his wake, and a flash of blinding light. Phoenix then transforms into a sparrow, and wings away from the fight. The explosion kills the Beast and singes Rex.

To everyone's eye, the Phoenix exploded into nothingness, and is now dead. Phoenix makes his way south, flying low over the trees, and is not noticed except for his blood causing small fires as he bleeds. Phoenix settles on a tree branch when he spots a camp of sea raiders and thinks better of stopping to put tears on his wound. Phoenix flies on toward the south. Late that night, Phoenix stops and applies tears to his injuries and stops the bleeding, but the wound is still wide open. Phoenix changes into his Phoenix form and flies deeper to the south in hopes of reaching the poison dart people.

Chapter

5

Phoenix is getting weak, and the loss of blood and the pain is taking its toll on him; Phoenix wanted to change to a sparrow so he could navigate the trees better, but the last time he did that, he almost became snake food. He transformed into an eagle and flew on to where the village had been located, and everything went dark, and he fell through the trees and brush until he landed hard on the ground. Just before he passed out, Phoenix changed to his human form. And from that time on, all was black.

Mara was in her old hut collecting the last of her things and was heading to her new home when she heard the crash of a body hitting the ground. She thought the raiders were back, so she hid where she could watch. Mara hears no other sounds; Mara decides to chance a look and happens to see Phoenix on the ground.

Mara was careful to use a large leaf to turn Phoenix over; she did not want to poison this man, at least not yet. Mara looked around to make sure no one else is about and then decides to build a travois so she can carry Phoenix to her new home. It didn't take her long to construct the travois from branches and vines with large leaves from some plant frons. Mara soon has Phoenix on the travois and struggles to drag him toward her new hut. As she is dragging him, she saw the trail she was leaving on the ground. After traveling fifty yards, Mara lets the travois down and goes back and brushes out the tracks to prevent the raiders from following her. Mara returns to her patient and checks on him before continuing her journey towards her new hut. After traveling a similar distance, Mara returns to brushes out the trail again when she hears people moving around in the area she had just left.

Mara returned back to where Phoenix lay and covered him under some brush; then she moved toward the noise; Mara changed into the small frog (poison dart) and hid in the bush next to the trail. Mara watched the sea raiders as they moved about, searching the area for signs of the people they were searching for. Mara steels herself. She may have to kill these men with her touch. Then one of the raiders calls out to come to the hut he entered. The two raiders near Mara return to where the third raider called from.

"Look, said one of the men, someone has been here. This hut had some furniture and boxes of dried plants, and now it's empty."

"Check around the hut to see if we can pick up a trail," said one of the other men.

They search the area and find only a footprint or two. The three men spread out and explored the area and all around the hut and find no other prints; they gave up on their search and decided to stay the night in the hut and return to the camp on the coast a few days away. Mara quickly returns to her patient and drags him away to her new hut, and she often pauses to brush out her tracks. By nightfall, she reaches her new hut, and she takes Phoenix inside and places him in the far corner of her room where she can keep an eye on him.

Mara starts a fire in her fire pit and gets water heating up. Mara covers Phoenix up, then makes some herbal soup with bits of snake for meat, and slowly feeds Phoenix. Mara turns to her patient and doses him with the antidote to her poison touch, then removes his clothes; Mara looks over Phoenix and sees the fiery blood flowing from the open cut in his side. Mara cleans his wound and, taking a bone needle and some gut, she sews it shut. Then Mara applies an herbal poultice to the wound and bandages him up. Then she looks him over to see if she needs to care for other injuries, and she finds none.

Mara checks his clothes and finds a knife and two vials of clear liquid. Curious, she opens a vial and tests it; Mara gets a feeling of good wellbeing and health; Mara goes to her patient and pours the vial of liquid in Phoenix's mouth and watches him. His fever breaks, and he falls into a restful sleep. In Mara's mind, this is a good thing. Mara lets her fire die out, and she lays beside Phoenix to sleep in case her patient should need her, she'll be right beside him. Both slept through the night.

Phoenix wakes and finds a strange girl in his bed in the morning. He pulls back the cover and finds he has no clothes on and pulls the blanket back over his body. Then Phoenix shakes the girl to wake her up. Mara wakes and stretches and yawns.

"You're awake? How do you feel?" asks Mara.

"Where're my clothes?" queries Phoenix.

Mara points to a small pile next to the door, "You can have them back in a while. They need to be washed."

"Who undressed me?" asks Phoenix blushing.

"I did," says Mara, "How else was I to treat your wounds?"

Phoenix looks to where the starstone sword had cut him, and it was bandaged and covered in some horrible smelling green muck.

"What is this stuff?" asks Phoenix.

"A poultice, it'll keep your wound clean while you heal. Now stop acting like a baby. What's your name? calling you hey you, will get very old."

"I'm called Phoenix, and your name?"

"PHOENIX! Our king?"

"Yes, I know I don't cut an impressive figure, but be that as it is, I'm that Phoenix."

Mara stammers "I'm called Mara."

"Thank you, Mara; you may have saved my life. I want to talk to the elder."

"You can't yet?" stammers Mara.

"Why not?"

"I've been exiled, and I may not return to the tribe. I tried to save a sea raider; he was a teenager. I gave him the antidote for our poison. Then he escaped, and the elder sent trackers to kill him, and they did. Then I was exiled they deemed me a danger to the tribe," whispers Mara.

"Ok, maybe it's for the best that I don't know where they are," said Phoenix.

"What do you want to see them for, Sire?"

"Mara, call me Todd; then, if we run into the sea raiders, they don't need to know who I am."

"Yes, Sire… I mean Todd."

"Now, Mara, please get my clothes washed so I can put them on."

"Oh, yes, right away." Mara collects the clothes and rushes to the stream a short distance away, where she washes Phoenix's clothes, returns a short time later, and hangs the clothes up to dry. Mara made breakfast, and they sat down on the mat to eat. Mara was in a state of shock at seeing her king. Due to the hot temperatures of the jungle, Phoenix's clothes were dried in no time, and he put them on, he wanted a bath, but Mara was insistent that he wait for his wound to close up to stop any infection.

"Todd, I pulled these vials from your pockets; what are they?"

"My tears, they can heal most wounds and sicknesses."

"Would they cure my poison touch?"

"Yes, and no. If you touch someone, I can heal them with my tears, but if you touch them a few days later, they will die from the poison, unless they got my tears again."

"I see, so it only works to heal once, while the antidote works indefinitely?"

"That's what Fenwick told me years ago."

"You knew my ancestor Fenwick?"

"Yes, we were fast friends. I save his grandchild with my tears, and he repaid me with the antidote to your poison."

Phoenix's wound was healing faster than she expected. Soon Phoenix was able to remove his bandage and then take a much-needed bath at the stream. Over the next few days, Mara has Phoenix doing simple chores to keep him moving, but not so much that he might tear out his stitches; in the late evenings, she'd get him to tell her about Fenwick and himself.

CHAPTER

6

It was late afternoon when Phoenix heard people talking outside the hut; he knew it was sea raiders from the accent. Phoenix whispered at Mara to change to a frog and hide under something, and he changed into his sparrow form to wait for the raiders to open the door to the hut. Phoenix shot out the door over the head of the raider, drawing his attention as he flew up into the brush, causing the men to lose sight of him. From the branches, Phoenix surveyed the men seeing only three men. Two with bows and one with a crossbow.

The raider with the crossbow turned back to the hut to investigate to see if anyone else might be hiding there.

Phoenix came up with the idea he could fly down between the men with the bows and take them by surprise. Phoenix flew down to within a few feet of the ground between the two raiders and changed to his human form, catching both men off guard. In a reactive response, they fired their bows at Phoenix, and he reverted to his sparrow form, and the arrows pass on either side of the sparrow, and the men hit each other one in the heart and the other in his right lung, and one raider cries out in pain. The raider inside the hut comes back out to see what's happened.

Phoenix was hopping along the ground away from the injured man. The raider that was dying, and he pointed at the sparrow and mumbled "he…" as he passed. The last raider aims at the sparrow when Phoenix flies off into the brush next to him and disappears into the treetops. The sea raider reenters the hut to finish searching. Phoenix drops down to the ground, picks up a bow and arrow, and calls out to the raider in the hut. Carefully the raider parts the curtain, and Phoenix shoots the bow, but the arrow misses its target.

"You had your chance, mate, now drop the bow and turn around, with your hands in the air."

Phoenix complies, "Now mate, where are your people?" The raider walks up behind Phoenix and prods him.'

"I don't know where they are, you caused them to move some time ago, and I was not informed where they went," states Phoenix.

"Then mate, you are no longer of any use to me." The raider checks his bolt and prepares to fire the bolt into Phoenix's heart.

Mara changes from frog to human from behind the raider and grabs the man from behind across his face with her hand. The man struggles free only to scream out from the poison coursing through his system, causing him pain than death. Mara drops to her knees and cries. She had never killed anyone before. Phoenix moves to her side helps her up, and moves her into the hut.

Phoenix removes the dead men a short distance back into the jungle and returns to Mara. She looks up as he enters, with tears running down her face. "I've never killed anyone like that before. The raiders, I never knew they could be so ruthless. The elders were right to exile me."

Phoenix wraps his arms around Mara and consoles her for a time.

"Mara, we must leave here."

"Where can I go where I won't kill some innocent person with my poison."

"Right now, I don't know! I can take you someplace where you will be safe for the time being."

Mara wiping her eyes, looks up and asks, "Where is that, Sire?"

"My grandfather's cottage, in the north. I need a place where I can plan my war. I'll keep you safe, Mara."

"What of my things, will I have to leave them behind?"

"What would you bring, Mara?"

"All my herbs and books."

"How much longer before I can leave here?"

Mara opens Phoenix's shirt and inspects the wound, and it is all but healed up. "You could leave tomorrow."

"Good! the raiders will send more to look for the ones we just killed; you'll not be safe here anymore. You'll have to come with me. Gather your herbs and books, dress warmly. It's cold where we're going. We'll need some food. It'll be a long flight to where we're going."

Mara wipes her face and sets about selecting the herbs she wants, and she collects the books about the plants and what they were used for. They eat in the quiet of the night and sleep fitfully, not knowing if more raiders are lurking about. Phoenix moves Mara and her things out into the clearing in the morning. For the first time in a while, he changes to the Phoenix. He can feel the sun's power again; it felt great to be whole again. He scoops up Mara and her large bag, then wings his way into the sky, then heads north, passing over places where no one has ever been so he can keep his presents of being alive secret. It takes a week and several days to get home at his secluded cottage, with frequent stops to sleep and eat.

Phoenix lands at his grandsires cottage and drops off Mara. "We're here, Mara; you'll be safe here; tomorrow, I'll take you to my cottage down in the valley to see where you'll wish to stay."

Phoenix opens the cottage door and ushers Mara into the house. Phoenix takes Mara to the small bedroom where his mother slept.

"Mara, you'll need to change your clothes; please change into one of my mother's dresses; there are shoes and such for you to put on next to the dresser."

"Todd, what is a dress, and what are shoes?"

"Mara, do you have any antidote?" queries Phoenix.

"Yes."

"Good! I'll be right back. I know someone who can help. Please stay in the house until I return and have the antidote ready," commands Phoenix.

CHAPTER

7

Phoenix leaves the cottage, changes into a falcon, and flies to his mother's house, where he meets with one of his adopted daughter's great-grandchildren. Phoenix knocks on the door, and as it opens, his granddaughter explodes into his arms with hugs and kisses on his face.

"Your alive!" screams Kimi.

"Yes, Kimi, I'm alive, but let's pretend I'm still dead."

"If you say so, Phoenix!"

"Just call me Todd; now I have a big favor to ask you."

Letting go of her grandfather, "what do you want me to do?"

"Change into a falcon and follow me to the smithy."

"Why?"

"I'll explain after we get there."

Ten minutes later, they both land in the front yard of the smithy, and they change back into their human forms.

"Kimi, wait here, and I'll be right back." Phoenix enters the cottage, collects Mara's antidote, and returns to Kimi. "Here, drink this, and follow me into the house."

Kimi looks at the clear liquid and swallows it down, and she follows her grandfather into the house. "Todd, why am I here?" asks Kimi.

Mara walks out of the bedroom, "You're here to help her put on some clothes, she is from the deep south, and she knows nothing of our northern ways," states Todd.

Kimi looks at Mara. Mara has raven black hair, deep brown eyes, smooth skin with a deep tan color. "Where is she from, Todd?"

"Mara is from the deep south, she is from a tribe called poison dart people, she is poison to touch, and anyone who does will die. That's why I had you drink the antidote," says Todd.

"Does Mara speak our language?" queries Kimi.

"After a fashion, I speak your language," states Mara.

"Todd thinks I need to dress like you; I'm not sure why?" queries Mara.

"Mara, follow me. I'll explain as best as I can. It'll keep you warmer here in the north, and it won't be so revealing," comments Kimi.

"Is there something wrong with how I dress?" asks Mara.

The women move back into the bedroom so Kimi can help Mara find some clothes to wear. Phoenix goes outside, and he changes into an eagle and flies off down into the valley to hunt up something for dinner. As he flies over the stream, he spots several large trout, and, in an instant, he swoops down and snags a trout out of the water, then flies back to the cottage.

Phoenix cleans the fish and takes it into the cottage, where he starts a fire to cook the fish. Phoenix spits the fish and turns it over on the fire, and puts some of the seasonings he has on the fish as he cooks it. Phoenix sets the table and puts the cooked trout on a platter. When the two women leave the bedroom with Mara dressed.

"Wow! Mara, you dress up nicely," said Todd.

The complement pleased Mara, "Are you pleased, Todd?" asked Mara.

"Very much so," said Todd.

Kimi covers her mouth as she smiles. Kimi suspects that Phoenix likes this exotic woman. Kimi knows that Mara seems to be taken by Phoenix. The whole time Kimi is dressing Mara, Mara would ask if Todd would like how she looked. Kimi seeing that Phoenix had caught dinner, decides to leave and return home, leaving the two alone. With a promise to return tomorrow, Kimi steps out and changes into an osprey, and fly's home.

"Todd, I have been meaning to ask you, who is Alana?" asks Mara.

"Where did you hear that name Mara?" asked Todd.

"From you, when you were with fever. You kept calling out her name," mentioned Mara.

"She was my wife, but she died of old age six hundred years ago," relates Todd.

"Oh, I'm sorry I asked," said Mara.

"It's ok, Mara; one needs to remember then move on. I miss her, and I'll always will," answered Todd.

To change the subject, what fish is this? I've never seen it's like before," asks Mara.

"It's called a trout. It's a cold-water fish; I guess you'll encounter many differences here in my culture," says Todd.

"You mean like all these clothes?"

"Mara, you may find them cumbersome now, but in a few weeks, when the season changes, you'll be glad you have them; now, let's eat before dinner gets cold," suggests Todd.

Evening changed into darkness; Mara went to Pam's old bedroom, while Phoenix took his grandparent's bedroom. After a few moments, Mara returned to the fire in her garment she wore in the jungle.

"Todd, should we sleep together as we did in my hut or like we did on our travel here?" queries Mara.

"Ahh... No, it wouldn't be proper. Follow me; I'll show you how to cover up in bed."

Todd leads her to his mother's bedroom, Todd helps Mara to bed, and then pulls the covers over her; then, he leans down to kiss her forehead.

"What was that, Todd?" asked a puzzled Mara.

"It's called a good night kiss; it's a custom here in my land," muses Todd.

Mara looks at Todd and smiles. "Are there any other nice customs like that here in your strange land?" asks Mara.

Chapter

8

Todd leaves and closes the door to Mara's room. Phoenix retrieves a map from a cupboard and sits down to study it. He marks all the places where he has encountered the sea raiders; in a few days, he'll do a recon along the east coast to see where other sea raiders' forces are, then back to the south, then west. He'll recruit others to help him as he takes back his kingdom.

Back at Castle Phoenix, the people there are driven into slavery, and Rex (Devlin) makes sure Jacob receives the full brunt of being his personal slave. Jacob is always with Rex and is never allowed to leave his side. Jacob is sent on useless errands and is frequently beaten. Rex liked to dress in Phoenix's clothes and use Phoenix's apartment. If Rex disliked Jacob's clothes, Rex would punish Jacob. Jacob hates Rex (Devlin), and in his mind, Jacob has killed his new master many times over. Jacob also feels sorry for his people; he had no clue how good they all had it under the Phoenix's rule. Now Jacob wishes the Phoenix had lived, and now they must endure under the rulership of the guild masters and the sea raiders.

Phoenix decides he must damage the sea raiders so severely in their own country that they can't mount a counterattack when he starts his campaign in his own country. Phoenix will then return after destroying the sea raider's ability to return to Phoenix's country. Then he would begin in the remote places of his country and destroy the sea raiders, then work his way slowly toward the southern castle, then onto castle Phoenix where he'll confront Rex for the last time.

Phoenix falls asleep at the table, and late in the night, Mara wakes him up, guides him to his bedroom, and gets him into bed. Mara decides to get into bed with Phoenix and keep warm at his side. In the morning, Phoenix awakes and finds Mara asleep next to him, and he grabs his clothes and gets dressed. Later, when Mara got up.

"Mara, sit down here. She does. You can't just come sleep with me; we're not married."

Mara giggles, "we are married according to my custom."

"How I never mated with you," exclaims Todd.

"I left with you; according to my people, that makes us a mated pair," claims Mara.

"In my culture, that doesn't qualify; it takes witnesses and others to cement a mated pair," explains Todd.

"You don't want me?" whispers Mara.

"I didn't say that; it's just a bit fast for me; I admit I like you."

Mara keeps her head down and smiles; she may not be able to stay with her people. Maybe she can make a new family like her great grand ancestor Fenwick did.

"Mara, you'll need to understand. I can't give you any children. I'm a eunuch; I've no stones to make you pregnant, so if you marry me, I can give you no family," explains Todd.'

"Oh! I didn't know," cries Mara.

"I'll tell you what, Mara, we can talk this over when I have my kingdom back and I have driven the enemy from my shores," says Todd.

"So, where do I stay? I can't return to my village. I've been exiled," cries Mara.

"You'll stay with me here where I can protect you and everyone else," states Todd.

"Alright, I'll obey your wishes," says Mara.

Mara returns to her room to sulk, but she follows the Phoenix's culture from that time forth. Mara struck up a deep friendship with Kimi and learns all she can about the local customs and culture.

CHAPTER

9

Phoenix starts his war; he left Mara in Kimi's care while he changed into his Phoenix form and flew east to cross the ocean. Phoenix flew to the sea raiders' land across the sea (Called Randal). Thanks to Alana's memory, the Phoenix burned out all the shipbuilding places and towns. Then Phoenix burned back the forests for ten miles along the river and ocean so he can cut the supply line of wood so the sea raiders couldn't supply people or supplies to build more ships to invade his land (New-Land). Then Phoenix flew back to New-Land back across the western ocean.

Phoenix's next goal is to destroy all the ships on the western sea than along the east coast of New-Land; the sea raiders will be trapped in New-Land where he can kill them once and for all. Starting up on the northernmost part of the coast of the eastern sea, Phoenix burns every boat he can find and all the raiders who oppose him— setting his people free from the guild master's clutches.

Phoenix settles down in the town or village he has just set free and talks to the people there. He finds a few people who can help him free the rest of the country. They're a mix of people who can change into birds or some form of a four-footed animal, such as a large cat or wolf-like animal. Phoenix has the people head inland toward Castle Phoenix. They're also to seek out and destroy any sea raiders as they go. Phoenix wants to keep the knowledge of his being alive a secret for as long as he can after he organizes the men and women who want to help. Phoenix pushes on to the south along the coast, destroying all the sea raider ships and as many armies of the sea raiders he encounters to free his people from the tyranny of the sea raiders and the guild masters.

Phoenix sees the sea raiders break up and flee inland to try to get away from the destruction at each village or town the Phoenix cleanses. Then Phoenix finds men and women willing to chase down the raiders and kill them for what they did to them when they enslaved the people. The poison dart people help out in killing off the raiders in their territory, using blowguns with poison darts. Phoenix continues to the southern jungles setting his people free and enlisting their aid to surround the southern castle to recapture it. Soon the raiders are so few that they cannot sail their ship (s) away back to their own land of Randal.

Phoenix arrives at the southernmost camp of the raiders to find that the poison dart people have all things well in hand. A couple of the raiders were being soundly punished for the crimes of hunting and killing the poison dart people. One man was strapped to a tree, and the dart people smeared tree sap all over him, and they left him for the sugar ants to consume. Another man was stripped of his clothes and staked down for the scavengers to finish killing him and eat him down to the bone.

Phoenix thought of burning them to ash, then thought better of it. He thanked the elder of the poison dart tribe for their help. Phoenix asked if he could meet with him from time to time without giving away their new location. The elder agreed that meeting here would be good. Just send up smoke, and the elder would come. Phoenix takes the elder's hand then says goodbye to his friend.

Phoenix flies north to the southern kingdom. When Phoenix was a day away from the southern castle, Phoenix changed from his Phoenix form to a falcon to fly to the nearest farmhouse; Phoenix lands in a tree to watch. Then Phoenix changes to a sparrow to move around the castle and its farming fields more efficiently.

Chapter

10

At the same time, back at Kimi's cottage, the women started their day. As luck would have it, two sea raiders are traveling toward castle Phoenix to warn them that the Phoenix is still alive. When the sea raiders spot the cottage, they decide to steal their food and anything of value. They pound on the door, and Kimi opens it to ask what they want. When the older of the two sea raiders leers at Kimi, we're hungry; they push past Kimi. Mara is still in her room getting dressed when she hears the commotion at the door.

"Now you'll give us some food!" demands the sea raider.

Kimi moves to the pantry to cut some cheese and meat to give them when the older man decides he wants more than just-food. He pulls Kimi down onto the floor and starts tearing away her clothes. The younger man helps to hold her down until Mara enters the room in her nightdress. The younger man lets go of Kimi to attack Mara; Mara offers no resistance. Mara says, "You don't want to do this," she warns.

The young man says, "Oh, yes, I do! I've not had a woman in a good long while," as he tears away her dress and grabs at her bare skin, then he cries out in pain then dies. "I told you; you didn't want to do that" Then Mara turns to the older man, and he grabs a knife to slash at Mara, and as he leaps toward Mara with his knife at the ready. Kimi changes to a panther and rips out his throat before he can get close to Mara.

"He tastes disgusting," spat Kimi. Then at the front door, another knock; Mara answers, "yes."

"Are you alright? we tracked two sea raiders here, and we wish to capture them."

Mara steps back and ushers them in. "You mean these two?"

"Yes, I see you can take care of yourself. Blake, come in here. We need to take these dead sea raiders out of here. Where do you want us to bury them?" asks the leader.

"There's a deep ravine behind the house. Toss them in there. The scavengers will take care of them," says Kimi.

"Blake, you heard the ladies," said the leader.

The men pick up the bodies, dump them in the ravine, and return to the house.

"We dropped them into the ravine for you; before we go, may we trouble you for some food? We've not eaten for a few days," said the leader.

Kimi rummages around the pantry and cuts up some bread and cheese, then she adds some sliced meat to the sack and gives it to them. Then tells them of the well at the back of the house. Kimi ponders what to do next, then decides to make up another sack of food and gets out a special harness to hook it to. Then directs Mara to change into her frog form then get into the open bag after Kimi transforms into her panther form. Once Mara changes into her small frog form, she hops into the sack. Kimi takes off after the men. They thank her and rush off in the direction of castle Phoenix.

Kimi feels that she and Mara can help.

Phoenix scouts around the southern castle to see what the sea raiders and the guild masters have done; sure enough, they have enslaved his people. Phoenix flies to the far edge of the field, drops to the ground next to the man working in the field, changes to his human form, and crouches down so he'd not be seen by the sea raider guard on the far side of the field.

"Do you know who I am, sir?" whispers Phoenix.

"No! Should I?" says the working man.

"I'm Phoenix, the king."

The man starts then recovers his motion. "You can't be the king. He was killed."

"Tell me can anyone do what the king can with fire?"

"No."

"Then watch." Phoenix turns his palms up and causes a small fire to appear.

"Majesty, you do live!"

"Yes, now why have you not thrown down this tyrant?"

"They hold our family at sword point. If we do anything, they will kill them."

"Where do you live?" The man stops, leans against his hoe, wipes his brow, casually points to his home, and then gets back to work hoeing.

"I'll set your family free; then I'll work on the other families."

"Best speed to you, Sire." Phoenix smiles and changes back to a sparrow and flies off to the man's home working in the field. Phoenix lands on the open window sill in his sparrow form and pecks at the seeds. There Phoenix looks into the house and sees the sea raider standing next to the woman and taking liberties he shouldn't be doing while the children are tied to their chairs. The woman pushes back and tries to fight him off.

Phoenix flies into the house and changes into his human form. Phoenix clears his throat.

"I believe the lady doesn't want to be manhandled by you," states the Phoenix.

The sea raider turns with his knife drawn. "Who's going to stop me, you?" yells the sea raider.

"If I must, I can and will." The raider lunged at Phoenix, and Phoenix danced out of the way, then grabbed the man's arm and burned it, forcing him to drop his knife. Before the man can recover, the woman sticks a knife into his back, killing the sea raider.

"I'm sorry you did that. I'd like to have questioned him, but he had it coming," said Phoenix from what I can see.

The woman turns with her knife to face Phoenix. "Who are you before I stab you?"

Phoenix holds up his empty hands. "I'm Phoenix, the king."

"No, you can't be; the guild killed him." She raises her knife when Phoenix lowers his hand over the dead sea raider and turns him to ash. She drops her knife, then drops to her knees and starts crying. "We had no hope, and now you're here again," she grabs Phoenix's leg. "Thank you, sir."

"Now stop that, young lady. Get up, free your children, and get into the woods to hide."

"What of the others?" as she wiped her tears.

"I'll get them; you just get your children to safety. Is there a place where you all can meet?" asks Phoenix.

"Send them to the holler; they'll know where that is."

"I'll see you later," said Phoenix.

"What about the men won't they be in danger?" she asks.

"Don't worry, they'll be safe enough; all they want is for you to be safe.

CHAPTER

11

The woman takes her children to the back room, then helps them out the rear window. They make their way to the woods; she guides the children the few miles to the holler to wait and hide.

Phoenix changes back to a sparrow and flies out the door and onto the next house, where he sees that they are clustered together. Phoenix flies to an open window then has to leave right away as a raider throws his food out the window. Phoenix passes through the open door and into the beams holding up the roof. Where can he watch what's going on below? Two men watching this woman; I wonder why? He muses.

One of the raiders tries to take liberties with her person when she wheels the pan in her hand and cracks it on the Raider's head, knocking him to the ground. His fellow partner is laughing, then draws his knife. "Missy, put that pan down and step back." At that point, Phoenix drops to the floor to resume his human form right behind the Raider with the knife.

"You're saying?" asked Phoenix.

The Raider reacts quickly to the voice of the strange man behind him. Phoenix has no wish to kill this man yet heats all the metal the man is wearing, causing third-degree burns on his hands a torso. The Raider at the woman's feet starts to stir, and with a smile of satisfaction, she bashes his head again, killing him.

"Well done, I'm Phoenix, and I'm here to free the people."

The woman raises her pan, "The Phoenix is dead."

"I have been told that; here, let me show you," Phoenix passes his hand over the dead Raider and turns him to ash. "Do you believe me now?" asks Phoenix.

"Yes! Please save my husband," she begs.

"I intend to; who is he?" asks Phoenix.

"He is the regent of this land."

"He's your husband; what he told me of you is pretty accurate."

"What has that man said about me?" she glares.

"How pretty you are and how much of a temper you have."

Megan is unsure if she should be mad or take it as a compliment. Phoenix turns away from Megan to see the Raider lying on the floor. Phoenix wakes up the Raider, who's in great pain "tell me how many sea raiders are here at the castle." The man spits into Phoenix's face.

"Too bad, I guess I'll leave you to the tender mercies of Megan here," she approaches with a butcher knife and passes it over his face, and he spills his guts about the army and how many sea raiders there are; he even tells of the spies that have been planted here.

"Thank you for being so good as to give up the information. Megan, he's all yours."

Magen plunges the knife deep into the Raider's heart, killing him instantly.

"Megan, what animal can you change to?" asks Phoenix.

Megan changes into a golden eagle, flies out the open door, and heads to the holler to meet up with the other women and children. Phoenix continues his covert actions and frees all the households on the castle's west side. Soon the men are marched back from the field as evening falls, they are under the guard of the sea raiders. In his sparrow form, Phoenix watches as the men arrive at the first house.

The leader calls out orders to the men guarding the family.

No one responds to the call. The leader has two men detach from the formation to check the house. Phoenix lands behind the leader and transforms into his human form. He presses a knife to the side of the man in charge.

"Tell your men to lay down their arms!" hisses Phoenix.

One of the men transforms into a sea bird and heads for the castle to get help when a golden eagle grabs the bird in midair and snaps its neck.

"Anyone else feels lucky enough to get away? No, ok, men, your families are safe, feel free to fight back," commands Phoenix.

The fight doesn't last long; all the sea raiders are killed except the leader. Phoenix turns to the leader, "How many men are here at the castle?" The man doesn't answer, so Phoenix prods him with his knife. "How many men!" commands Phoenix.

The leader tells him two-hundred men, "Good, where's the regent, and is he still alive?"

"The regent is in the throne room, and he's still alive," stammers the leader.

"Ok, I will turn you over to these men; I hope you were kind to them."

The leader screams, and it's cut short as the men take some of their vengeance on him. Phoenix explains his plan to the men, "the west side has been set free. We need to free the North and South sides of the castle," states Phoenix.

"If we all work together, we can free the rest of the people outside the walls; what say you?" asks Phoenix.

One of the men piped up, "We are with you, Sire," all the men agreed. Phoenix sketches out a plan to liberate the people to the castle's north. With some more help, the people on the south side of the castle could be rescued quickly; many of the women were more than eager to fight with their men. Phoenix tells them he's going to start inside the castle. Itself, we need to accomplish this before dawn.

They decide who goes where, and all the people who can transform into owls will patrol the sky in and around the castle to keep any birds from flying to the northern regions to warn the other guild masters of a rebellion here in the south. The people select a cottage to invade. Then as quiet as possible, the enslaved people kill the sea raiders as they go. Phoenix changes to an owl and flies to the castle wall; then changes to a sparrow and flies into the open smithy. Then up into the rafters to observe what's happening.

From his vantage point, Phoenix sees the sea raider, a blacksmith working away at the forge with the owner of the smithy chained to the billows, and he is being forced to pump it for the sea raider as he forges another sword. The hate in the owner's blacksmith eyes says it all; he'd kill the Raider. Phoenix drops down to the floor and changes to his human self. The sea raider grabs a nearby sword; Phoenix takes one down from the self, tries it, to find its balance, and turns to face the sea raider.

"Well, puny man, they call me Terrible Black; what do I call you after killing you?"

"You may address me as Phoenix."

The Raider lashes out at Phoenix. If the blow had landed, it would have cleft Phoenix's head. Phoenix dances out of the way and slashes Black's arm. Black charges Phoenix getting more enraged as Phoenix dances out of the way and slashes Black in various places, bleeding him. Then, on Black's sword's final thrust, Phoenix dances around the sword and thrusts his sword into Black's throat. Amazed and looking down at the sword stuck in his neck, Black drops to his knees, gurgles his last and dies.

Phoenix searches Black's body and finds the keys to the shackles holding Justin. Justin stands there staring at Phoenix in amazement. "You're King Phoenix?" stammers Justin.

Phoenix laughs, "Yes, I'm your King, and no, I'm not dead. Now, where is the regent? I want to save him next."

"Like me, he is chained to the throne, where the guild master displays him for all to see."

"I believe it's time to set him free; what do you think, Justin?"

Justin takes down a sword, "lead the way, Sire, I'll follow."

Phoenix and Justin walk out of the smithy and survey the walls, then locates the spies and the few archers on the walls. Phoenix burns down the men before they can shoot or raise the alarm. Then with Justin, they enter the castle keeping to the shadows. They make their way to the throne room; it's empty of people except the regent chained to the throne. Phoenix gently shakes the regent awake. The reagent reacts quickly and has Phoenix by the throat before realizing who was waking him up.

Phoenix grabs the regent's hand, and pry's it free from his throat. Justin kneels next to his cousin, "Cousin, we're here to free you and everyone else," whispers Justin.

Phoenix helps regent John to his feet, "Do you want me to remove your chains?"

"Not, all of them, just the parts holding my feet and hands together; when I finish with the guild master, he'll remove them for me," the regent rumbles.

"John, where are the sea raiders?" asks Phoenix.

"They're in the banquet hall, swilling down all the food and drink," the Regent grumbles.

"I'll take care of them; do you want the guild master?" asks Phoenix.

"Yes!" John changes into a half-wolf and half-man form and stalks up the stairs to where the guild master took over the Phoenix's apartment. John breaks down the door and rushes into the flat, and grabs the guild master by the throat. John pulls the guild master face to face.

"Unlock my chains!" growls John.

The guild master fishes around in his robe and pulls out a knife, but before using it, Justin chops the guild master's hand off, still holding the knife. John rakes his claws across the guild master's face. And pulls him face to face again, "unlock my chains before I slash your guts open and feed on them," growls John. With fear plastered on his face, the guild master pulls the keys out of his pocket and unlocks the chains. Still holding on to the guild master, they head down to the banquet hall to meet with Phoenix. All the piles of ash speak of what Phoenix has done.

John holds the guild master by the throat, and Justin binds the arm with a thong to stop the guild master from bleeding to death.

"Thanks, John. Guild master, I want answers if you don't give them to me; I'm sure John here can make your current life more painful. Now, where have you staged your main force?" queries Phoenix.

Phoenix walks to the wall, takes down a torch, and walks back to the guild master. The guild master says nothing; John rakes his claws across the guild master's back, eliciting a scream of pain. The guild master says nothing.

"You're still bleeding; let me cauterize your arm." Phoenix holds the torch flame to the arm stump. The guild master screams and passes out. "John, he belongs to you; I've learned what I wanted," said Phoenix.

"Sire, he didn't speak," growls John.

"Which tells me they've taken over the communication center where everyone sends messages. This is where they'll concentrate their forces; that will be the next place I'll take over."

"What do you want me to do with this scum?" grunts John.

Phoenix turns to John, "it's your regency he invaded, have a trial and do what you want with him," states Phoenix.

"Thank you, Sire." John hands the guild master over to Justin and changes to his human self.

"John, do you have a clean place where I can sleep for a few hours, I've been up for the last three days, and I'm tired," said Phoenix.

"This way, Sire, I'll have some food sent to you." John leads Phoenix to a room that hasn't been used. Then John turns to go to the kitchen to order some food for his King. On the way there, a golden eagle lands on his shoulder. John winces as the great bird grips his shoulder.

John turns to the bird, "I am well, my wife." He stands still as she drops to the floor, changes to her human form, and hugs her husband. John leads them to the kitchen, orders food for King Phoenix, and sees its delivery.

"How is the war with the sea raiders doing?" asks John of his wife.

"We have them captured, none have escaped," said Magen.

"How many are alive?" queries John.

"I'm not sure one, maybe two," says Megan.

Laughing, John rubs Megan's head and hugs her, "Justin bring the guild master, and let's go see the people," commands John.

"Yes, cousin," as Justin drags the guild master across the floor and to the castle landing.

The people had gathered to see if all was well in the castle, "Everyone, we have our kingdom back, and we're now free from the sea raiders and the guild masters, all thanks to our King the Phoenix. He'd be here, but he was so exhausted that he is now asleep. I thank you for your help in freeing our loved ones. Now go home and get some much-deserved rest and food. Tomorrow we'll meet and make plans to prevent this in the future. Good night my friends!"

"Cousin, what do you want me to do with this guild master?" queries Justin.

John pauses a moment in thought, "lock him in the dungeon, the one with no openings and a solid door. We'll decide what to do with him."

Justin calls on a couple of his friends, and they drag the guild master down the stairs to the dungeon, then toss him in, and lock the door.

CHAPTER

12

In a couple of days, after Phoenix catches up on some much-needed sleep, Phoenix comes down to the main hall to find John and Justin with several key people setting up some plans to protect themselves in the future from such an invasion by the sea raiders and guild masters. Having listened to their plans, Phoenix asks about the communication center that regent Mary set up six hundred years ago. "Can it provide some timely warning?"

"Good question, Sire, but we've not heard from them in several months," states John.

"Let's go see the guild master; maybe he can answer some of my questions," said Phoenix.

They all follow Phoenix down into the dungeon to question the guild master. It turns out that the guild master wouldn't answer any questions. It turns out the guild master tries to kill John with a knife. Causing Justin to kill the guild master with his knife.

"Too bad you had to do that, Justin; I'll not get what information I was hoping to get from the guild master," sighs Phoenix.

"I'm sorry, Sire."

"Don't be, Justin; he needed killing anyway. Now I must travel to the communication center to see if I can take it back."

"Are you sure, Sire, that they, have it?" asks John.

"I believe it's a good bet, you haven't received any messages for some time, and the guild master was willing to die before we could force him to tell us," Muses Phoenix.

"What do you want us to do, Sire?" asks Justin.

"Look for and stop any sea raiders between here and castle Phoenix; I'm going to the west to free the people there, then I'll move on to the communication center, and when I have it secure, I'll move on to castle Phoenix for the final battle for my kingdom."

Refreshed and fed, Phoenix bids the people goodbye launches into the air in his Phoenix form, then heads west to free his people from the grip of the sea raiders and restore his kingdom. Phoenix takes a several days to reach the furthermost ranch to check up on his friend. As Phoenix approaches, he changes to a sparrow so he can enter the ranch unnoticed. Out in the pasture, his friend Carlton is tending to his animals. Phoenix drops down to the ground and changes to his human form.

"Carlton is all well with you and your family?" queries Phoenix.

"Yes, Sire, all is well; why do you ask?"

"No sea raiders here?"

"No Sire, no sea raiders are here," said Carlton.

"Carlton, be careful; they'll be coming here soon."

"Thanks for letting me know, Sire; I'll be ready."

"I must travel to the east now to ensure my people aren't under duress. Bye Carlton, I'll come to visit when I can stay longer," says Phoenix.

Phoenix launched into the air as an osprey and headed east to the next ranch after Phoenix left Carlton. Two strange men in chain mail approach Carlton. Carlton watches the men approach him, and he leans on his quarterstaff as if he has difficulty walking. The two men ask where the master of the land is, and Carlton says that he is the master. The two men laugh, and one draws his sword and says, "where is your family?"

Carlton points to the large building and indicates they're there. "Why did you want to know, friend?"

"We're not your friend. We're your new master! We'll hold your family hostage." Both men laugh.

Carlton, without a word, stands up straight, spins his quarterstaff like an expert, and disarms the man with the sword. Then the sea raider's friend grabs his bow and an arrow; before he can set the arrow to bow, he too is knocked to the ground.

"You were saying about hostages?" asks Carlton.

Both men roll to their feet, and one draws a knife, and the other his sword, and they circle Carlton with the intent to kill him. Carlton keeps his staff moving, and before the man with the sword can move in, he finds his hand broken as Carlton flicks his staff. Then he hits the man with the knife in the face knocking him out and the man with the broken hand rushes Carlton with his drawn knife. Carlton jabs him with his staff in the solar plexus, breaking the man's sternum and driving out his breath. The knocked-out man comes to and tries to change to a raven and fly off, and Carlton bats the raven out of the air before he can get away, killing it. The man on the ground tries to change to a rat and scurry away, and Carlton lands a blow on the rat's body, killing it.

Mad at killing the men, Carlton says, "What a waste." Then Carlton goes off to tend his ranch leaving the dead animals to the scavengers.

Phoenix approaches the next ranch, and he manages to intercept the raiders before they reach the next ranch turning the men to ash. Soon Phoenix has all the west of his kingdom free. Phoenix moves on to the communication center. Phoenix realizes he has to be most careful here. He doesn't want any sea raiders flying out from here to warn castle Phoenix that he's still alive. Phoenix wonders if this may be too late already, for that thought, after all, he has cut off the north, east, and the south. The guild masters have to suspect something is going on.

Phoenix finished with the western lands of his kingdom. Phoenix moved on toward the Communication center; at first, he flew as the Phoenix until Phoenix got close, then he changed to an osprey and flies close to the building. Phoenix wants to see how the enemy is holding the center. Phoenix changes into a sparrow to blend in with the other local birds.

Down in the central chamber sat a guild master directing the sea raiders and Phoenix's subjects as if conducting a symphony, receiving and sending information and orders via the people who can fly. Phoenix flies around like a sparrow staying close to the ceiling beams so he can sit and look down on the activity below. Phoenix watches for some time, not giving away his presents. Phoenix spots one of his friends receiving his orders, and he changes into a hawk to fly off to deliver a message. Phoenix flies out just ahead of the hawk, and when they get away from the building, Phoenix changes into an eagle, catches the hawk, and forces him to the ground in a secluded area. Phoenix changes to his human form, as does the hawk, the man who was the hawk punches Phoenix on the jaw knocking him off him, and he jumps to his feet, ready to fight on.

Phoenix laughing and rubbing his jaw, holds up his hand, "Brad, hold on, it's me, Phoenix, your friend."

Stunned, Brad stops in the mid movement to throw another punch, "Wha... Phoenix!"

"Yes, old friend, it's me."

"They said you were dead!"

"Good, they're supposed to believe that so I can work in the dark, so to speak, and take back my kingdom."

"So, you're the one they are looking for?"

"They are looking for me?"

"They are keeping things quiet, but we have lost communications from the east and the south. they are trying to find out what's going on," stated Brad.

"I guess it had to happen sooner or later. How many sea raiders are here?"

"They have twenty stationed here to keep us in line and another ten flying to some of the main areas. But of late, the fliers have not returned, and the guild master who is in constant contact with castle Phoenix is showing concern."

"Brad, can you contact enough of our people who are birds of prey to catch or kill the sea raider birds."

"You must be kidding. All of us would kill them if we knew our families were safe."

"None of you live here at the center, do you?"

"No, Sir, we live in the area we come from," stated Brad.

"Good, the center and castle Phoenix are the last two areas that need to fall; all the other areas have been liberated," says Phoenix.

Brad smacks his fist into his open hand and smiles, "Sire, your wish will be my command, and that'll be one command I look forward to," growls Brad.

"When can we start, Brad?"

"Is now too soon, Sire?"

"Not at all; hide here, Sire; I'll spread the word."

"How do you plan to do that, Brad?"

"Watch the center, Sire; you'll see it in action."

Brad flies off to the center, Phoenix changes to a sparrow and flies back into the center. He was watching from the rafters. It doesn't take long, and all hell breaks loose. Phoenix's subjects start a brawl that gets everyone involved. The guild master is standing on the dais shouting orders; as he watches his men being taken down, the guild master looks like he will change and escape during the melee. The guild master begins to change into some bird's form; Phoenix pounces upon the guild master stopping his change.

Phoenix forces the guild master down and, with a flaming hand, threatens the guild master with instant death unless he returns to his human form.

The guild master in his human form, "Who are you!" he screams.

"Who else? I'm Phoenix, the king."

"You can't be; I saw you die. I watched as you were destroyed."

"That was a bit of show I put on to make you believe you had killed me."

"You gave your word; you wouldn't use your power."

"I lied; after all, if I had won, you were poised to kill me anyway, so I chose deception."

"Then all your people will then be killed."

"Really? What do you think I've been doing? I have destroyed all your ships and army. Up and down the coast! This is the last refuge of the sea raiders, and as you can see, it's back under my command."

The guild master spits in Phoenix's face, "So what are you going to do brand me and then exile me. I see how far that got you with Rex."

"Here, since you expect my brand," Phoenix takes out his metal seal and heats it to a yellow color. He waves it over the guild master's face and plunges the brand onto the guild master's right cheek. The guild master screams.

Phoenix turns to the men standing about him and the guild master, "No, I'm not the one who will kill your guild master. Men, he belongs to you; you decide what to do with him."

"No, you can't do that. They'll kill me."

"You should've considered that before you came to my kingdom."

The men took the guild master out of the center; it was not done very gently. By the time they got to the forest's edge, the guild master had suffered a broken arm and a leg. To keep him from flying away,

it took a few hours to kill the guild master, but the men were taking
all the torment the sea raiders did to them out on the guild master.
When he was dead, they left him for the scavengers to remove what
was left of him.

Chapter

13

Now all that was left to do was recapture castle Phoenix, and he knew that the people he sent ahead had the castle surrounded, and they were ready to attack. Phoenix need only give the signal. Phoenix sent the people who could either fly or run on all fours, which would help him take back castle Phoenix from the west side of his kingdom, and he flew with them. In his eagle form. Phoenix and his army arrive at castle Phoenix in a few days to begin his final war at home.

Phoenix hopes that the people coming from the east are at the castle in hiding, waiting for his signal to begin to advance upon the castle to take it. Phoenix flew over the castle in his sparrow form, and from his body, he sent up a flare to start the attack. The fliers came over the top of the wall taking out the sea raiders who manned the walls, while the four-footed troops flooded into the castle via the open gate. Separate skirmishes broke out all over the place. Kimi and Mara entered the gate and went directly to the smithy to check on Orion. (Kimi's friend).

In her panther form, Kimi burst through the door to the smithy and managed to place herself between Orion and the sea raider. The sea raider raised his sword to strike at Kimi when from behind the raider, Mara had changed to her human self and tapped the sea raider on the shoulder, causing him to spin around and grab her by the throat as he was about to plunge his sword into Mara the sea raider drops his sword. The sea raider then starts clawing at his neck and gasping as if to breathe before he dies.

Amazed, Orion looks at Mara and is afraid of her. Kimi changes to her human self and locates the key to Orion's chains, then sets him free. Without hesitation, Orion pushes Kimi to one side and throws a knife in the direction of Mara, to the shock of both Kimi and Mara. The blade missed Mara and struck the sea raider in the heart, sneaking up on Mara, ready to kill her. Orion grabs his sword, charges out the smithy's door, and joins in on the fighting.

Inside the castle, Phoenix flies about in his sparrow form. And locates Jacob chained to a wall next to the throne. Jacob is weak from lack of food and water. Phoenix frees him and helps him to stand up.

"Sire, I thought you were dead?" croaks Jacob.

"No, Jacob, I'm quite alive."

"I saw you die," exclaims Jacob. "We all saw you!"

"No, you saw what I wanted you to see; now, let's get you to safety."

"No, Sire, all this is my fault; I don't deserve to be freed," croaks Jacob.

"I see! we can talk this over later when this is all settled, Jacob."

With his last ounce of strength, Jacob pushes Phoenix to one side and takes a knife in his chest intended for the Phoenix. Phoenix turns and burns the sea raider to ash, Phoenix turns back to Jacob, and then kneels to pick up Jacob's head.

Jacob reaches up to touch Phoenix's face. "Forgive…" and Jacob dies.

Phoenix screams for Rex to come out. Rex leaps out the door with the starstone sword in his hand; Rex is slashing the air, trying to keep Phoenix at bay. Rex advances on Phoenix, pushing him back down the corridor. Phoenix backs up and is enraged. Phoenix leads Rex through the halls burning all sea raiders to ash as he finds them, it doesn't take long, and Rex wonders why Phoenix didn't burn him down to ash the whole time.

When Phoenix vanishes, Rex thrusts at Phoenix, trying to skewer him on the sword's point. Phoenix wants Rex alive, so he pulls the same trick as before a flash of bright light, changes to his sparrow form, and flies behind Rex. While Rex recovers his sight, Phoenix returns to his human form right behind Rex and relieves him of the starstone sword, then uses it to pin Rex to the wall.

"Give up, Rex, the castle has fallen, and you've lost!" states Phoenix.

"You think so? I've men all over, not to mention an army on the east coast. We'll retake this kingdom," shouts Rex.

"Wrong, Rex, we've destroyed all your men and ships. I even flew to your country Randal across the sea and destroyed all your ships and the shipyards. You lose Rex."

"You can't; it was all planned out; you can't do this!" screams Rex.

Orion and several people came charging into the apartment.

"Sire, are you ok?" queries Orion.

"I'm fine, Orion, march this filth to the coast; I suggest you break his arm; he can change into a raven or a rat; I'd not want to have him escape on his way to his execution," says Phoenix between clenched teeth.

One of the men with a mace struck Rex's shoulder and broke it, causing Rex much pain.

Phoenix pushed up close to Rex, "you will die this time, Rex, and I'm going to use your method to do it; as you die, remember this, I'm going to conquer Randal and bring it under my rule as well. Orion organizes a march to the eastern sea. I want Rex to arrive there alive. I have a special death planned for Rex," states Phoenix.

Orion assembles a small army to march Rex to the eastern sea, knowing it will take several weeks to make the trip. While Orion picked men and supplies to make the trip, Kimi and Mara decided to go with them. Before they leave, Mara gives Orion a vile of liquid.

"Orion, you must drink this potion. It'll protect you from my poison touch," says Mara.

Orion looks at her, he opens the vile, and downs the potion all in one gulp. "Not bad. Will this allow me to touch you now?" Orion asks.

"Yes, be sure to tell the others not to touch me; I don't have enough potion for everyone."

"I will, Mara," said Orion.

It takes a few days to get the party moving on their way to the east coast. Phoenix sent people who could fly to keep track of their progress so he can fly to the coast to execute his judgment on Rex. In the meantime, Phoenix needs to bury the dead. And respect everyone who died in the retaking of his kingdom. Phoenix wants to let everyone know that Jacob saved his king's life and gave his own life in the end. Jacob will be accorded heroes send off. Phoenix flies to the east coast four weeks later to intercept the detachment escorting Rex to his execution.

"Sire, what do you want us to do with the prisoner?" queries Orion.

Phoenix looks out at sea and sees that it's at high tide. "Orion, we wait; we'll dig a hole for Rex to sit in with his head sticking out when the tide goes out."

"Are you sure, Sire?" queries Orion.

"Yes, Orion, it's a way they execute their criminals. By the way, did Kimi and Mara make it back home?" asks Phoenix.

"Yes, when we drew near their home, they left us," stated Orion.

"Good, they shouldn't have to see this," growls Phoenix.

Phoenix has his men dig a hole in the sand halfway between the sea and high tide. Then sticking Rex into the hole and fill in the sand up to Rex's neck at low tide. Rex pleads with them the whole time to let him go or kill him outright. Phoenix would hear none of this. If for no other reason than to watch Rex die for revenge. After Rex was buried, Phoenix sent the men back home; only a few stayed. Rex watched as the tide came in for four hours, getting closer and closer. Then as the water reaches his chin, he starts screaming. The next wave drowns out the screams, and Rex is underwater and drowns in the next couple of waves.

Phoenix flies back to Kimi's place with Orion clutched in his claw to check on Kimi and Mara. Phoenix lands in Kimi's yard and transforms back to his human form. Kimi and Mara burst forth from the house to hug Phoenix and Orion. Phoenix sees that Mara has a liking for Orion, and Orion likewise has feelings for Mara. Later in the day, Mara pulls Phoenix aside to tell him how she feels about Orion then asks if he would reconsider their bonding.

Phoenix smiles and consents to release their bonding. Phoenix wasn't sure if he wanted another mate at this time. Phoenix still hurts from losing Alana, his first wife, six hundred years ago.

"Mara have you any more antidote for your poison so that others won't get poisoned by accident?" asks Phoenix.

"No, I gave my last vile to Orion. If I'm to make more, I'll need to return to my hut in the jungle so I can harvest the plants I need to distill the potion," says Mara.

"Mara, when should we leave to harvest the plants, you need?" asks Phoenix.

"Soon, the plant's flowers will be in full bloom now and will only last a few weeks; then, we'll have to wait until next year," says Mara tapping her cheek with her left hand.

"Go explain to Kimi and Orion what we need to do, Mara. Tomorrow morning we'll leave." Explains Phoenix.

Chapter

14

Mara explains to Kimi and Orion what's going to happen. Both Kimi and Orion want to go along. Phoenix explains that it's not possible at this time, they'll have to travel very fast, and Mara will be wearing the only suitable clothes for traveling, Alana's leather suit. Plus, the narrow window of time to harvest the plants. In the morning, Phoenix and Mara, with a bag of her equipment, say their goodbyes, and fly off to the south to the deep jungles.

Orion leaves to return home just after Phoenix leaves, realizing that Mara will be gone for at least a month. Phoenix decides to fly straight through to Mara's old hut, and to make it easier, Mara ties herself to Phoenix's leg and goes into a suspended state to keep from eating. It helps fight off the cold as Phoenix flies very high in the sky, like above ten thousand feet in the air where the air is thin and the temperature is cold.

Days later, Phoenix lands at Mara's hut in the jungle. Phoenix carries her into it and places her on her sleeping mat. Phoenix forgers for some food, and when his hunger is sated, he picks a corner it the hut and falls deep asleep. A couple of days later, to Phoenix, it was just last night, or so it seemed to Mara it was just moments ago that she went into a suspended state then woke up. Mara shakes Phoenix to wake him. Phoenix stretches and asks how long he was asleep. Mara looks at him and shrugs.

"I don't know; I just awoke myself. Are you hungry?" asked Mara.

"Yes, I could eat a whole deer right about now," yawns Phoenix.

"Here, let me fix you something. Then I need to get up into the upper tree canopy to gather the needed flower for making the potion," says Mara.

When breakfast was over, Phoenix changed into an eagle, then scoops up Mara in her frog form, and flies up into the tree canopy. Phoenix looks for an opening to get above the trees. A snake-like creature tried to snag him out of the air. In response to the attack, Phoenix burns the creature to ash. Phoenix found an opening in the canopy and flew up above the trees. It doesn't take long, and Phoenix settles on a tree limb big enough to hold his and Mara's weight in their human forms. Mara and Phoenix change back to their human forms. Mara tells Phoenix to stay put and she'll gather the flowers.

Mara has the satchel filled to bursting with flowers two hours later. Mara and Phoenix return to the jungle floor, where Mara then makes haste to get back to her hut to start cooking the flowers down into a slurry. As the flowers cook, Mara tells Phoenix what to do when the slurry is finished so she can go out and collect other ingredients for the potion. Two days later, the brew is complete and needs to be stored. Phoenix had brought a case full of vials, and they took the time to fill each one and cap them with a waxy substance.

"Phoenix, we have as much potion as we can make for this year, and we have twenty vials from the looks of it. This should be enough to see me through until next year."

"Good, we'll leave in the morning to return to Kimi; we can take it in stages on the return trip," said Phoenix.

Mara agreed and gently packed away the case of vials into her satchel, ensuring they would not get broken for the return trip. As a precaution, Mara put four vials into her pocket of Alana's flight clothes. The following day after a hearty meal, they set out to return to Kimi's cottage passing through the southern castle.

Two days later, Phoenix lands at the southern castle to visit old friends and have a nice rest stop. Phoenix flies over the castle and makes a thunderous cry to let the people know he has arrived. The regent and his wife come forth from the castle to greet Phoenix. Mara is dropped off, and Phoenix changes his human form to greet his friends. The regent's wife reaches out to hug Mara. Mara pulls back, and Phoenix cries out to stop Megan before touching Mara.

"What have I done? I meant no offense," says Megan.

"No offense was given; if you'd touched her, you'd have died; she is a poison dart person," states Phoenix.

"Oh my, I've heard stories of such people, but I never believed they were true," said John.

"Mara, would you give them each a potion vital to protect them from your poison," requests Phoenix.

Mara takes two vials from her pocket and provides the king regent and his wife a potion vial. They are instructed to drink it down. After which, they can now touch Mara without dying. The regent leads Phoenix and Mara into the castle to get them settled, with special care to prevent anyone from coming into contact with Mara. The next few days pass without incident, and Phoenix and the king regent confer over what had happened with the sea raider invasion and work on a plan to counter another attempt by the guild masters and the sea raiders.

The biggest problem is the distance between the lands and kingdoms; if we could communicate fast enough to set off an alarm to ready our people for defense.

"John, you set up a way of communications to the south watching station and one to the northern castle, and in the future, we can prevent this from happening again," said Phoenix.

"Yes, Sire, I have a couple of men I know who can help set this up and run it with efficiency," said John with confidence.

"John, I'll leave this in your capable hands; Mara and I need to press on; I've some thinking and planning to do. I will conquer the guild masters and sea raiders and bring peace to us all. We'll be leaving in the morning John, thank you!" yawns Phoenix.

"For what, Sire?"

"For taking this task over, I know you'll accomplish it and make it work."

Phoenix and Mara turn in to get some much-needed rest before pressing on to the north. In the morning, John and Megan see Phoenix and Mara off on their journey. After two more days of flying without stopping sees them landing at Phoenix's cottage, and it's late in the day, Phoenix carries Mara into the cottage and places her in her bed, and Phoenix turns to his bed and crashes. Phoenix checks on Mara in the morning, and she's still in suspension. He realizes he's so hungry he could eat a whole lama.

Phoenix washes his face at the water trough out beside the yard. Then he launches into the air and flies down into the valley to hunt up something for breakfast. He sees a large salmon resting on a sand bar; Phoenix changes into an eagle. Phoenix swoops down, snags the fish, and flies back to the cottage to clean and cook his catch. Mara stumbles out of her room as the fish is cooking on the spit. Mara realizes that she, too, is hungry.

When breakfast is over, and the dishes are cleaned up and put away. Phoenix and Mara decide to walk to Kimi's cottage to help work the kinks out of their bodies. At the end of the hour walk, they worked out their stiffness of the last several days. When they reached Kimi's yard, she came exploding out of the front door to issue hugs and kisses. When the greetings were over, Kimi ushered them into the house so she could feed them, but they assured Kimi they had just finished a good breakfast of salmon, so Kimi settled on serving some tea and cookies.

Phoenix needed to make a trip to castle Phoenix to set up a new regent to replace Jacob. Then, he will travel across the eastern sea and free the sea raider people as he had done here. Phoenix hands each girl two vials of his tears and warns them to keep them safe. Kimi and Mara knew how valuable the vials were. Phoenix then left them to fly to castle Phoenix.

Phoenix arrives at castle Phoenix, and he changes to a sparrow so he can enter the courtyard unobserved. Phoenix flew into the smithy and assumed his human shape, catching Orion off guard in mid hammer stroke.

"Ahh... don't do that, Sire; you nearly scared a year's growth out of me," pants Orion.

"With a chuckle, sorry, Orion! I need to talk with you about installing a new regent to replace Jacob."

"Surely you don't mean me to do you, Sire?" asks Orion.

"No, you're not seasoned enough yet to be a regent. Maybe in time. For now, I need someone dependable and loyal," said Phoenix.

"Oh, that's easy, Sire; you want a shepherd named Ted."

"How so?" queries Phoenix.

"Ted settled a dispute between three landholders and showed them a better way to manage their land, where everyone gets better crop yields," said Orion.

"Ok, tell me how he did it, Orion."

"Ted helped the landowners set up a schedule for who would grow which crop, which prevented them from growing the same crop. They all now grow different crops. And they rotate who grows which crop, and he also set it up to let a landowner let his field lay dormant for a rest, and Ted would graze his animals on the land that was dormant so it would get fertilized. That farmer would provide help to whichever farmer needed help. His system seems to be working out, and others are beginning to follow his lead," said Orion.

"When can I meet this, Ted?" asks Phoenix.

"We can go see him now if you'd like to, Sire?"

"let's go see him!"

Orion leads the way; outside the gate, Orion changes to a panther, and Phoenix changes to a falcon to keep up as Orion runs off to the west. When they reach their destination Orion changes back into his human form, followed by Phoenix. They arrived in the area where Ted watches his flock. An hour later. Orion points to Ted, "Sire, that's the man you wish to talk to."

"Let's go introduce ourselves," said Phoenix.

Orion leading the way, walks up to Ted and gives him a greeting. Then introduces Phoenix, the King. Ted is beside himself, wondering why the King would come to see him.

"Ted, I hear good things about you and some of the things you have accomplished with your neighbors."

"What things have you heard, Sire?" asks Ted.

"Orion has told me about the agreement you worked out between you and the farmers and the benefit they're receiving."

"Oh, that, it was just common sense. Nothing more. It was a mutual help for us all."

"I'm looking for a man to replace Jacob, who recently died, my people need a good regent, and I'd like you to fill that position," said Phoenix.

"I'm flattered, Sire, but I have my flock to tend. Then I have the farmers to help as I promised I would."

"I see; you're a responsible person as well. As a regent, you only need to attend court a few times a week to attend to the realm's business. On the days you can't be with your flock, have the farmer whose land you are grazing on tending the flock."

Ted looks down toward the ground and rubs his beard in consideration. "Sire, you're as wise as I've heard. What you propose would work. Maybe I can get all the farmers and herders to work together. Yes, I accept. When will I start?" asks Ted.

"I'm holding court tomorrow; can you be there?"

"I'll be there, Sire," says Ted.

"Good! I look forward to introducing you as the regent. I will introduce Orion as your second," smirks Phoenix.

Orion starts to splutter, "but Sire, I don't have the sense to rule."

"Then, working with Ted, you'll get the seasoning I mentioned earlier." Phoenix and Ted started laughing and clapped Orion on the shoulder in a friendly fashion.

Ted remarks to Orion, "friend, no good deed goes unpunished." And they all laughed.

The following day Phoenix is holding court. Orion and Ted show up; the last to arrive is the scribe to record all that takes place for future reference. Phoenix takes the throne, and the first of his subjects show up. Phoenix turns to Ted and Orion and introduces them to the people that Ted is the new regent, and Orion is the coregent. At the end of that day's audience, Phoenix pulls Ted and Orion off to a secluded room to task them to set up a communication system with the south and a small militia to protect the realm from the very thing they had just fought with the sea raisers. They both agreed to do that.

Phoenix told them he'd be leaving at the end of the week and maybe gone for a couple of years. They asked where he was going; all he'd say was to prevent the guild masters and sea raiders from ever attacking this country as they have in years past. Ted and Orion let it drop. They figured that Phoenix would tell them when he was ready. Phoenix wouldn't be disappointed in Ted or Orion. They would rule well in his absents. Phoenix was sure he was leaving his kingdom in good hands. On the morning of the last day, Phoenix said goodbye and flew off to the east.

On his way to the eastern land (Randal) across the sea, he stopped by to see Kimi and Mara. He was well greeted, and he spent the day and night with them before he would continue his trip across the eastern sea. The whole day Phoenix answered questions about Orion from Mara and Kimi. In the end, Phoenix realizes that Mara was the one who was interested in Orion. To Phoenix's way of thinking, this was a good thing. Phoenix says his goodbyes to both girls in the morning and wishes them well.

CHAPTER

15

Phoenix launches himself into the air and changes from a hawk into his Phoenix form. Then Phoenix flies up high and heads out over the western sea for the three-day crossing. On the third evening, Phoenix lands on the river bank where he had landed years ago. He sets up a camp then has a meal of some dried meat he had brought. Phoenix drank the water from the nearby stream to slake his thirst.

That night Phoenix is going over what he has been moiling over in his mind since he retook his kingdom back from the guild masters. Phoenix would take over this country as he did a thousand years ago in New-Land. Phoenix would set the people free from the grip of the guild masters here in Randal. Phoenix was tired from the three-day flight over the sea. He fell asleep rolled up in his blanket. In the morning, he was rudely awakened by a couple of people jabbing him with the butt of a spear and the wet nose of a wolf sniffing his face.

Phoenix awakes with a start and sets up only to have a spear point pressing against his chest. "Well, sir, who are you, and why are you here on our land?" growls the man with the spear.

"I'm called Todd, and I just finished flying across the sea and landed here to rest. I'm sorry if I trespassed on your land," yawns Phoenix.

"Git up, Todd or whoever you are, you're going to go back to our village until we can think of what to do with you. Gip! Tie his hands behind his back."

Gip ties up Phoenix's hands and Phoenix decides to go along with them for now; in an hour, they have traversed the distance to the village. Where Todd (Phoenix) was presented to the leader who would decide his fate, or so they thought. The leader sent fliers and a couple of wolves to check over the area to ensure that Todd was not a scout for a possible attack. Once it's settled that Todd is not a scout, they put Todd into a storage hut for safe keeping. The leader has Todd tied to a post at the center of the hut. Later that night, a woman offers Todd water and some food. Todd drinks the water, but the food Todd passed on. The food looked a bit burnt and under done.

The woman then ate the semi-cooked meat as if she were hungry. As she ate, Todd looked her over; she was filthy. The ragged dress is so bad that it doesn't cover her very well. As she is eating the food she brought for Todd. She watches Todd and notices he is watching her. She misunderstands, and she takes off her dress. She offers herself to him, and Todd said no. She put her clothes back on. She left the storage hut and returned to her house and her bed.

Todd decides to burn his bindings off as he stands and stretches. Todd looks around; he finds a leather strap on a shelf. Todd sits back down and makes it appear as if he were still tied up to see what would happen. In the early hours of the morning Todd decides to fly back to his camp to get his pack and his starstone sword. Todd was wondering why the Gip and his friend left it in the first place. Todd changed into a sparrow and flew back to his camp to find the two men in question retrieving his pack and sword.

The two men saw the sword and started fighting over it; soon, they were rolling around slugging each other when Todd reached down and picked up his sword; then, he got their attention by stabbing the sword into the ground next to their faces, they stopped fighting.

"What are you doing here? Your tied up in the storage hut," croaked Gip.

"As you can see, I'm right here to claim the property you were going to steal," stated Todd.

"I don't know how you got loose, but you'll die now!" as Gip grabbed his spear and tried to stab Todd.

Todd (Phoenix), using his sword, cuts the spear into small sections and Todd presses the sword against Gip's chest; in the meantime, Todd knows Gip's friend has pulled a knife and is approaching his back. Before either man realizes, Todd spins around and, using the flat of his sword, hits the man behind him up alongside his head, knocking him out. Before Gip can react, Todd has his sword pressed against Gip's chest again.

"Now pick up your friend. We're going back to your village."

Grumbling Gip picks up his companion and staggers back to the village with Todd walking behind them so he can prod Gip from time to time. They reach the village, and Gip drops his friend and stands up. "What do you want me to do now, Todd?"

"Go get your head, man I want to challenge him to a duel."

"Todd, you don't want to do that. He'll split you from head to toe with his ax."

"I'll take my chances," said Todd.

"You're a fool; Fang has never lost a duel."

"Gip, go get him," commands Todd.

Gip walks into the village and calls out to Fang. Gip informs Fang he has a challenge in leadership. Fang appears with his huge ax, and behind him, a group of men with bows and arrows come boiling out of the longhouse.

"Who challenges Fang for leadership?"

Fang walks out to where Todd stands with his starstone sword at the ready. Todd doesn't move but in the back of his mind, (where do they grow these giants, I may have to rethink these challenges for taking over these people.) Todd muses.

"I challenge your leadership," states Todd.

"Who are you? Dog!" bellows Fang.

"I'm called many things, but here and now, I'm called Todd. I'll tell you my true name if you can best me in single combat," said Todd.

"Then stand ready, flea!" Fang charges Todd swinging his ax to deliver a blow that would split a man's skull.

Todd sidesteps the blow, spins around Fang, and delivers a stinging slap with the flat of his blade to Fang's face. Fang realizes he missed his mark, and in a greater rage, he faces Todd with another double-handed swing. Fang brings his ax down, striking the ground and not Todd. As Fang turns to face Todd, Todd has his blade pressed against Fang's throat.

"Fang yield or die," commands Todd.

Fang stands there, realizing he could die. Fang lowers his ax and steps back. Fang then gives a signal to his men. Several archers fire their arrows at Todd. Todd had expected this, and as the arrows closed on him, they were turned to ash in midair. Fang stands there with his eyes wide.

"Who are you? What sorcery is this?" Fang stammers.

"I'm Phoenix. Does that tell you all that you need to know? Now yield or die!"

"You can't be the Phoenix; that was a thousand years ago; the Phoenix is just a legend," states Fang.

Phoenix heaves a big sigh, then bursts into his Phoenix form and shatters the air with his thunderous scream, making everyone cringe and fall to the ground for fear of their lives. Phoenix returns to his human form.

"Fang, do you yield to me?" commands Phoenix.

"If I do, will you let us live?" quires Fang.

"I'm not here to destroy your people; I'm here to conquer you and set you free," said Phoenix.

"I yield to you! Phoenix." Fang turns to his men and has them stand down.

"Fang, call all your people out here the woman too," said Todd.

"The woman, why they're nothing more than slaves in our culture," complains Fang.

"They'll be slaves no more; they'll become like the woman of my land. You'll realize that women are to be prized as partners, not slaves," said Phoenix.

Phoenix spent the rest of the day explaining his new rules, which caused much confusion between the men and the woman of this village. The more mature woman picks up on what the Phoenix offers, and they explain it to the other woman. At the end of the next few days, the woman owns the homes, and the men learned how they are to treat them with respect. In a month, all the men and the woman are beginning to see the advantage of this new way of freedom.

In the next step, Phoenix gathers the men and women who want to learn to dance the sword, and he trains them; even Fang learned. This is a step in building his new army. Over time Phoenix returns Fang to being in charge of this village. Fang became Phoenix's friend and protector.

"Sire, I never knew living could be like this; I thank you for what you have taught us. We need to bring this freedom to the rest of Randal," says Fang.

Phoenix smiles and clasps Fang on his massive shoulder. "I intend to do that very thing, and your people will help me."

"How will we help Sire?" queries Fang.

"We'll start tomorrow; where is the next tribe or village?" asks Phoenix.

"It's twenty miles to the east of us."

"Very good; I'll do there what I've done here. You and your men will leave with me to get their attention."

"Where you go, Sire, I'll follow," said Fang as he pounded his chest with his fist.

"For now, yes! but in the future, I'll need you here to rule in my stead Fang."

"If you say so, Sire. The woman Mariam who is my wife is with a child she will deliver in a few months."

"All the better for you to return here to rule Fang, so you can teach your child to rule well."

"I'll call the men together, and the women who want to go fight the next tribe, we'll be ready in the morning," said Fang.

"I need to leave; Fang, I'll be back in a few hours; get everyone ready who's going."

"Yes, Sire."

Fang goes off to gather the small army. Phoenix launches into the sky and flies to the next tribe to see how much of a task it'll be to confront them. Phoenix changes from his Phoenix form into a sparrow so he can check out the tribe; it doesn't take long to find the man in charge.

Chapter

16

He's not as large as Fang, but he acts as if he'll be more difficult to convince to give in. Phoenix flies back to his current base of his operations.

In the morning, all the men were gathered and changed over to wolves. As a wolf pack, they run to the next tribe to subdue it. Phoenix flies just ahead of the pack, and Fang keeps the men in line when they arrive; they don't attack the tribe or any of their people; the men are for show and to draw the men with the head man out into the open.

Fang positions the men and women in a formation. Phoenix shows up in his Phoenix form and thunders out his challenge, and the head man presents himself to ask what Fang wants. Phoenix changes to his human form and stands in front of his small army with his sword.

"I challenge you to a duel for the right to rule here! What is your response?" challenges Phoenix.

"Take this band of men and leave while you can, or I'll destroy you and them," said Red-Hand.

"I take it you are fearful of my challenge," said Phoenix.

"I fear no man, not even Fang, standing behind you," shouts Red-Hand.

"That's good, then you'll have no trouble fighting with me then! Or are you afraid to fight me?" challenges Phoenix.

"Ok, I'll fight; remember, I gave you a chance to walk away. I Red-Hand accept this challenge!"

The fight didn't last long; at the end, Red-Hand was kneeling on the ground, both cheeks of his face red from being hit by the flat of Phoenix's sword, and several other places were sore. In one instance, Phoenix knocked Red-Hand's sword from his hand and then handed it back to him. At the end of two hours, Red-Hand yields to this Phoenix person.

Red-Hand has his men stand down, expecting Fang's men to take his spoils. Red-Hand and his tribe become shocked when that doesn't happen. Instead, Phoenix hands back Red-Hand's sword.

"We're not here to take anything from you; I'm here to free your people and give them a better way of living. Fang brought his men to help you adjust to the new rules."

"New rules?" asked Red-Hand.

Phoenix turns Red-Hand over to Fang and his men. It helps speed up the process of intergrading the new way of life. At first, it was confusing and strange, but it took hold, and everyone got along. It wasn't long, and they were ready to take on the next tribe. Fang and Red-Hand became fast friends; both men were great followers of Phoenix.

Each time Phoenix faced down a tribal leader and intergraded that tribe into his way of ruling, the word of his conquest and freedom spread ahead of him so that when he showed up, the people gave in to him before he could even issue a challenge. Phoenix had conquered every tribe south of the main river within the year.

Word of Phoenix's conquest has reached the northern tribes and cities of the guild masters. The guild masters set about to gather their armies to fight this conquest of this usurper from the south.

Phoenix was involved with his new conquest of the sea raiders. Back home, things were in grave danger. Plague broke out, and the people under Ted with Orion were trying to figure out where it came from and what they could do to stop it.

A week earlier Mara is getting restless and tells Kimi that she wants to go to castle Phoenix. Kimi laughs and says, "You just want to see Orion."

"Am I that transparent?" says Mara.

"Yes, you are," giggles Kimi.

"I'd like to go to the castle too; I have a few friends I'd like to visit. Mara, we can leave in the morning let's get our stuff ready for traveling."

"Really! I'll take my new dress. Kimi, you don't mind if I woo Orion, do you?"

"No, he's like a brother to me, not a lover or prospective husband," says Kimi.

"Ok, I'll get my stuff ready for you to carry," says Mara.

As the women get ready for their trek to Castle Phoenix, a messenger from the southern castle is on his way to the communication center and he is very tired, hungry, and thirsty. He spots a stagnant pond as he flies north, then circles back to land. Like a bird, he finds some small fish in the pond, some insects, then just a drink of water before he takes wing to get back to the communication center to pass on his message from the southern regent to the northern regent. The messenger contracted the plague from the pond.

Before shutting down the communication center, the plague had gotten out to the southern kingdom and Castle Phoenix via messengers. The messenger which contracted the plague passes on his message; then, he goes to the barracks to get some sleep. In the morning, one of the people in the barracks went to wake the man. He was covered in pustules and had a high fever. They brought in a healer to look after the man, and soon others were suffering the same sickness, even the healer.

A month later, Kimi carrying Mara in a suspended state, arrives at Castle Phoenix to find their way barred. The guard tells Kimi what's going on, and he's to keep people away for their protection. Kimi decides to go to her friend's home in the valley so she can revive the small frog who is Mara. With Mara revived and the news about the plague revealed, Mara riffles through the pack to find her book (A book that her ancestor Fenwick wrote nine hundred years ago on sicknesses and cures).

After checking with her book, Mara sees that this plague is not mentioned, but Fenwick found that the bark of the green sap tree seems to cure most sicknesses. "No! Mara exclaims, that'll take at least two months to harvest the bark and return."

"Mara, what's wrong?" queries Kimi.

"This tree only grows in the deep south where I lived; without Phoenix to fly me there, it'll take too much time to save anyone."

"No. cries Kimi; Orion has the beginnings of the plague and may die."

"Ok, Kimi give me one of the vials of Phoenix tears you have; that'll help enhance the potion and stretch out tears healing property for more people. Then I need the fastest flyers we can get to take me to the jungle to find the tree. I'll need three strong fliers to carry back the bark to the southern castle and come back here," says Mara.

"I'll have the people you need here in the hour," says Kimi with conviction.

An Osprey with three other people who can fly as eagles arrive; they will be carrying the bark back from the jungle to castle Phoenix. Mara writes down the directions to make the potion they'll need so Kimi can make it up as soon as the bark arrives. Mara attaches the Phoenix tears to the note so Kimi won't use it for anything else but the potion. Mara was just about to give the directions on how and where to go when five other people show up; they were from the wolf clan who helped Phoenix in the last skirmish with the sea raiders.

"Why have you come?" asks Mara.

"We heard what you will do; we would help," stated the leader.

"You cannot fly; how can you help?" asks Mara.

"You don't know about wolves, do you?"

"I guess not," confessed Mara.

"We can travel vast distances without sleep; we may not keep up with you on the wing, but give us the location, and we'll be there, and we'll bring back the bark to Castle Phoenix."

Mara drew a map of where she lived and told them not to drink any water from ponds or stagnate water, only from moving water. Kimi returns, and Mara gives her the note she wrote. Mara provides the eagle with people and the Osprey with a potion vial to protect them from her touch. The wolves set off on the trip. After saying her goodbyes, the Osprey is fitted with Mara's sling, where she will sleep the whole trip. The Osprey launches with his precious cargo, followed by the eagles.

It takes a month to reach her hut in the jungle, and she missed the trip there, being in a suspended state the whole time. The man who was the Osprey followed his directions and revived Mara a day before the eagles arrived. Once Mara was fully awake, she located the trees she needed and showed the men how to harvest the bark. Only take a little of the bark so they wouldn't kill the tree. As the men peeled the bark, Mara searched for and find seeds for a chance of growing the trees later. Mara also took the opportunity to gather other seeds from other helpful plants.

When they were finished harvesting the bark, the wolf clan showed up, so they could collect the bark and return to Castle Phoenix. The wolves left as soon as they had the bark and headed back home. Mara had ground up the bark and loaded up the three eagles. Mara changed to a frog and got back into her pouch so that they could leave for the southern castle. All the birds got to the southern castle in another week again; the Osprey revived Mara from her suspended state. Mara walked into the castle to begin making the plague potion.

The men who brought her to the castle stayed well away from the people there, and no one argued with them about it. They set up a camp and stayed there, sleeping, waiting for the return trip to Castle Phoenix. Mara made the bark potion and gave it to the worse case, and they improved, but it didn't cure. Mara then emptied the vial of Phoenix tears into the solution and gave it to the same person, and he became well in a few hours. Mara took the potion herself after she started feeling sick, and she, too, got well.

Mara went to the fliers and gave them a potion to drink to make sure they would stay well. Mara and the recovered people helped feed the potion to others until everyone was cured. The king regent was so thankful for Mara and her help, he wanted to provide them with a banquet, but due to time, Mara declined and soon left to return to Castle Phoenix. Mara was concerned about her friends Kimi and Orion.

The wolf clan returned in less time it took them to get to the deep jungle. They ran day and night to return as soon as they could. They even had to leave a couple of their clan behind. The clan was so exhausted from the trip that they collapsed at Kimi's friend's house waiting for them. Following Mara's directions, Kimi ground up the bark and boiled it, and when it cooled, she poured in the vial of tears from Phoenix and went to the castle to give the plague victims a dose of the potion.

Kimi gave the wolf clan the potion, and they ran to the communication center to help the people there. Like at the southern castle, the sick recovered; they pitched in to help, and soon, everyone who was still alive recovered from the plague. Within a week, everyone was cured. Now the weeping and grieving begin.

Mara returned, and she went to look up Kimi and then Orion. Mara found him well. She hugged him and wouldn't let him go; she was afraid for his life. The regent entered the smithy to find and thank Mara for what she did, he reached a hand to take her hand, and Kimi smacked his hand away.

Shocked, "Why did you stop me from taking Mara's hand?" asks Ted.

"She's a poison dart person. You would have died if you had touched her; her poison is that fast."

The regent drew back, "I didn't know; I meant no offense," said Ted.

"Here, drink; this potion it protects you from her poison," said Kimi, handing a vial to the regent.

Ted drank down the potion and was confused, "Can I touch her now, or do I have to wait?"

"You can touch her now; you'll be safe," said Kimi.

Ted reached out his hand and closed his eyes as he took Mara's hand, "Thank you, Mara, you saved us all from this plague, you may ask anything of me, and I'll grant it for you if it's within my ability to do so."

"You're welcome, your majesty; right now, I'm happy to have served you and Phoenix. Now I must try to find out how all this started," stated Mara.

"Well, I think I can help there, said Ted; one of our carriers was traveling from the southern kingdom, and he stopped at a stagnant pond for a meal and a drink."

"I suspected as much. You need to thank the people who went with me, especially the wolf clan. They were tireless in traveling to the jungle and returning home with the bark," said Mara.

"I'll see that the wolf clan gets commended for their efforts and the four fliers too," said Ted.

Mara turned to Ted and Orion, "I need to sleep. It has been long several days. Being in suspension is not as restful as a goods night sleep," yawns Mara.

Orion guides Mara and Kimi to his living quarters at the back of the smithy, "you women can sleep here; I'll sleep in the smithy next to the forge," said Orion.

Ted smiles, knowing how Orion feels about Mara, and he turns and heads back to the castle. Tomorrow will be a busy and sad day, and Ted is thinking (I will have to deal with all the grief from burying the dead, but be happy the plague has been ended.) The new day shows up as Ted is dealing with burying the dead and saying how sorry he and the Phoenix would be about the loss of life and friends. Now we must see that this doesn't happen again in the future.

Mara heard the speech and got an idea of what she could ask Ted for. Land and a building to grow her plants. Mara would need a scribe to duplicate the book she had from Fenwick. Mara talked to Kimi and Orion about her idea, and Orion said he would put in a good word with Ted. In the morning, Orion went to Ted, and they discussed Mara's plan to grow her exotic plants and duplicate her ancestor's book of plants and potions.

Ted agreed to all Mara asked for. Mara was given the land next to Orion's smithy so his forge could be used to keep her plants warm. Ted also agreed to have the roof of the building plated in glazed glass to act as a way to get more heat, and sunlight Mara might need to grow her plants. A new scribe was given to Mara, who she protected from her poison so they could be close together. This was the start of creating a new profession of a medical nature.

CHAPTER

17

Phoenix had a vast army who followed him, and they came to the main river, which divided the northern tribes from the southern tribes. When they reached the river, the guild masters had assembled their armies at the ford in the river to prevent Phoenix's armies from crossing and entering their lands. Phoenix calls upon the leaders of his tribes and commands them to gather the army back from the river but stay in sight of the opposing army. "I'm going to challenge the guild masters to combat for the leadership of their armies," said Phoenix.

The leader's Fang and Red-Hand cautioned that the guild masters are full of tricks and lies. Phoenix assured them he knew of their treachery and would be as sly as they are. Phoenix walks to the edge of the river, then explodes into his Phoenix form and shoots up into the sky, issuing his challenge in a thunderous scream bringing the armies on the northern shore to their knees. This brought out the guild masters from their tent. Phoenix lands several yards from them then changes back into his human form with his sword in hand as the last shimmers of his flaming form fade away.

Phoenix reissues his challenge "I challenge you for the leadership of this army and the city!" The leader of the guild masters faces Phoenix "You challenge the guild masters? You don't have the authority to issue a challenge to us, Phoenix!"

"So! Are you going to back down from the challenge guild master? What do you think the sea raiders will consider of your lack of participation after the challenge has been issued?"

The leader looks about and sees the sea raiders watching, then realizes that the sea raiders would rebel against their rule if they refused. "I'll accept your challenge, with the caveat that we can call on a champion, and you can't use your power to burn him down. If you lose, you'll leave this land and not return."

"I accept, except for one thing, that the fight is a fair fight with no treachery on your part. If you follow this, I'll abide by your terms. If you break your word, I can use my powers," challenges The Phoenix.

"I accept your terms; the fight will take place in an hour," said the guild master leader.

"I'm not going anywhere; call up your champion," commands Phoenix.

An hour later, the guild master has brought out one of the most giant of a man Phoenix has ever seen. Phoenix watches the large man, and he seems to move strangely. Phoenix stands at the ready with his starstone sword. Then it comes to the Phoenix, this man's chimera is a bear, which means excellent strength, but he'll not have the speed. Phoenix recalls the Dance-master's training and how strength can be countered.

The bear-like man changes to a hybrid man and bear, and he wheels a double-bladed ax and wears body armor; the champion walks up to Phoenix, who is waiting in the middle of the field. The champion stands in front of Phoenix. The champion placed his ax on the ground with both hands on the weapon's handle. All Phoenix had been his starstone sword and no armor.

Phoenix decides to get the champion angry. "Not only are you ugly, but I wonder if you'll last the whole fight?" taunts Phoenix.

The bear-man slams down his ax right beside Phoenix, "You won't last ten minutes under my attack, little bird!" growls the champion.

"I'm ready!" shouts Phoenix.

Phoenix brings up his sword to parry the bear's first attack. The ax slides off Phoenix's sword and is deflected to one side. Angry, the bear brought down his other fist, and Phoenix danced out of the way. With each attack, Phoenix draws blood from the places where the armor can't protect the bear-man. The flight lasts an hour, and the bear-man is slowing down.

Phoenix will hate to kill this man-bear, but this duel is to the death. Phoenix ducked and danced past the bear's attack, and Phoenix slashed the back of the bear's calf, causing the bear to limp then fall; the bear had so many cuts, and his blood was flowing, making him weak. The bear makes his final attack, and Phoenix dances in close and thrusts his sword upward into the bear's neck and brain, killing him instantly.

The Phoenix is covered in blood, but it's not his own. Phoenix walks up to the guild master leader, "you lost the challenge. Now abide by our terms!" says Phoenix with hate.

The guild master can't abide losing, so he throws a poisoned knife at Phoenix; Phoenix deflects the blade with his sword, then he burns down the guild master leader to ash. "Anyone else feels lucky enough to try to kill me, or will you abide by the terms?" queries Phoenix.

The next guild master stepped up and said we'll honor our terms. Phoenix changed to his Phoenix form, launched up into the air, and told the army to stand down. He had won the combat for leadership. Then Phoenix lands and gestures to the men who were closer to arrest the guild masters until they can be escorted to the coast in the east and shipped out. The new army complies with Phoenix's command. They arrest the guild masters.

The city falls to the Phoenix without a fight. Phoenix assigned new leaders and turned everyone free. The people became drunk on freedom. Soon the word spread throughout the land in the north, and the tribes came to him to become free and join the Phoenix's army. The following two cities fall without a fight, and the people rejoice to be free of the guild masters. In some cases, the guild masters are hung or beheaded before Phoenix approaches the city gates.

A great city on the coast is the last to fall, and it came at a high price. The guild masters still alive had raced to gather there and convince the people that the coming army would butcher them and their families. The misinformed sea raiders prepare to repel the Phoenix's armies. The castle has a hidden pier where the guild masters launch a couple of ships, while the people who lived in the castle had all their attention focused on the invading army, which was stationed just out of bow reach. The guild masters sneak away to the ships then set sail for their last refuse, an island several months away in the middle of the ocean.

The guild masters will take time to prepare and return to reconquer the land and somehow defeat or kill the hated Phoenix.

Phoenix approaches the city gate and walls in a loud voice asks the people to surrender. Phoenix pleads that they surrender. He is answered with a curtain of arrows which he burned to ash in midair. Another curtain of arrows is their answer, and the arrows are met with Phoenix's power and turned to ash in mid-flight. Phoenix turns to the gate and burns it to ash, killing a hand full of men and women to his sorrow. The city men gather at the entrance to repel the invaders, but the invaders don't charge. They hold their position; only Phoenix stood there.

"Look, you people of the city, I don't know what lies the guild masters have told you! We're here to liberate you, not kill you. If I wanted to kill you, I could've burned you all and your city to ash. I won't do that!" shouts Phoenix.

A leader steps forward from the mass of people at the gate, "What are your terms?" he demands.

"Turn over the guild masters, and learn what freedom can give you," answers Phoenix.

"What will that be? Trade one master for another?" queries the leader.

"In a way that will be true, you will dump the guild masters and step into their place," said Phoenix.

"I don't believe you!" said the leader.

Phoenix turns to his army and calls the leaders to come forward; a dozen men step up to where Phoenix stands. "Men, tell them what you now have in freedom."

The men speak up and tell them the freedoms they now enjoy. They didn't show up to fight. We came to show you what you can have in freedom! While the leaders under the Phoenix speak, the leader dispatches men to collect the guild masters, only to find that they fled in the last two ships for their Island. The leader then decides to surrender to Phoenix. To the city's amazement, they learned the truth about Phoenix's freedom and the lies of the guild masters.

Phoenix questions where this Island is where the guild masters came from; they're not sure of the distance, merely the direction. Phoenix leaves the leaders and people to work out this new freedom. Phoenix launches into the air in his Phoenix form. Phoenix soars up as high as he can so he can see far out to sea. As it happens, Phoenix locates the wake of the two ships, and he soars in that direction until he spies the ships. Phoenix quickly changes to his falcon shape until he gets close enough to be seen, then he changes to a sparrow in hopes of landing on the ship without being noticed.

Chapter 18

Phoenix lands in the rigging of the lead ship; from his vantage point, Phoenix watches the crew, and he sees a way to take refuge in the hold of the ship. Down in the hold, Phoenix finds some clothes, and he changes into them so he may blend in with the crew, but to make sure he's not discovered so quickly in the clothes he stole, Phoenix changes to a sparrow and flies to the trailing ship and blends in with that crew.

What would trip Phoenix up is that he doesn't know how to work on a ship. Phoenix knows nothing of rigging or any other part of how a ship operates, so he locates the smithy then offers to assist the blacksmith. Using his father's name Todd, he tells the smithy that he stowed away to get away from the war. The smithy doesn't believe that Todd can help him. He tells Todd to take over what he is forging and finish it. It was a cleat that had been broken.

Todd takes the cold metal, heats it, forges it to shape, sets about to heat treat, and then tempers the cleat so it won't break again.

Intrigued, the smithy asks Todd where he had learned his skill and knowledge about working with metal. Todd indicates that he worked for his grandfather at his smithy, and they lived in a southwestern tribe.

"Alright, Todd, I'll tell the captain you came on with me as an apprentice; I'll throw you overboard if you cause me any trouble," growls Fenwick.

"Thank you, what is your name?" asks Todd.

"Todd, you call me master, but my name is Fenwick."

"Yes, master," said Todd.

"Now, young Todd, what did you do to that cleat to make it so tuff?" asks Fenwick.

"Master, it's called hardening, then tempering," says Todd.

"Show me how you do it," requests Fenwick.

Todd takes a piece of metal and heats it until it reaches the proper color, then quenches it to make the metal hard. At this stage, the metal is somewhat brittle. Todd takes the metal back to the forge and reheats it up to a different color, then quenches it, which gives it a temper that makes it less hard. Fenwick is interested; he'd never been taught this metalworking method.

"Todd, you've taught me this day. What other processes do you know you'd teach me?" queries Fenwick.

"Fenwick, if I understand this trip will take several months, we can teach each other our skills. I'm willing to teach and learn what you know." Todd holds out his hand to shake Fenwick's. Fenwick looks at Todd's hand and takes it to show his agreement. Over the time at sea Todd and Fenwick become fast friends. Fenwick learns new ways to forge metal, and some of the knives they turn out are great works of skill and art. Fenwick and Todd had the knives sold as fast as they finished making them. It was a prosperous exchange for both men.

One morning, the Island is sighted, and Todd comes up on deck to see the Island; then, shortly, Todd returns to the smithy in the hold, Todd tells Fenwick goodbye, and wishes him well.

"Todd, where are you going?" asks Fenwick.

"I have other business here on the island Fenwick, and you need to forget me." Todd takes Fenwick's hand and shakes it for the last time. Todd returns to the upper deck then, jumps overboard, changing to a sparrow, and flies to the Island to explore and see what he might do to stop the guild masters from leaving the Island.

Phoenix changes to his falcon form and flies around the Island. One thing he notices is they don't have much by way of trees, so if he destroys the two ships in the harbor, he can maroon everyone here on this Island. This idea is very appealing. It will keep him from turning the whole Island into a burnt cinder. Phoenix can destroy the ships as he leaves the Island for the four-day trip back to the mainland of the sea raiders country, Randal.

Before Phoenix can make the trip, he needs to get some rest and a good meal for the long journey. Phoenix is looking for someplace where he can sleep undisturbed. He is flying over a small grove of fruit trees when he hears screaming, and some men laughing. Phoenix hates it when men force a woman or abuse them. Phoenix drops down below the trees, changes to a sparrow, and flies among the trees until he finds where the commotion is coming from, and what he sees makes his blood boil. A woman is being pushed about and beaten up.

Phoenix changes to his human form then draws his starstone sword and clears his throat to get their attention. Two men were holding the girl by her arms, and the third man was about to start cutting the girl with his knife. All three men looked up to see a person offering a challenge.

"Who are you, stranger?" asks the leader who held the knife.

"I'm called Phoenix," Phoenix spat that out with venom.

"Is that supposed to mean something to us, stranger?" said one of the men holding the struggling girl.

"Probably not, but it will!"

The man with the knife drew his sword and approached Phoenix as if he should be frightened. The man lunges with his sword and follows up with his knife. Phoenix dances away and hits the raider's hand holding the knife with the flat of his sword knocking the knife from his hand. The woman was still struggling to get away when the man holding her slugs her knocking her out. Then he threw her to the ground and draws his sword to help his friend engage the stranger.

Phoenix toyed with the men for a short time; then, he knocked one senseless with the flat of his sword. The remaining raiders turned and beat feet away from the fight. Phoenix bends over the woman to see how hurt she is. Gently Phoenix checks her over and saw she was not hurt beyond a few bruises. Phoenix starts to pick her up when she grabs his knife and stabs the man trying to stab Phoenix in the back.

"You fool, you don't leave your enemy alive here; you kill them!" she said.

"Thanks, we best leave here," said Phoenix, "Before his friend returns with more friends."

Phoenix helps her to her feet, and she leads them away from the spot. They move down into a grotto where she has a hidden cave, she moves the bush that covers the entrance just enough to push by, and Phoenix follows her. Once past the entrance, she leads him deeper into the cave, and they reach a rather large rock blocking the way. The woman pushes on one side of the rock, moving to one side. She ushers Phoenix inside, and she pushes the stone back into place.

"We'll be safe here for the time being. Why did you stop to help me?" she asks.

"I heard you scream and went to investigate then saw you being abused; I got angry and decided to stop it," said Phoenix.

"That was stupid; the people here don't like me and fear me; they call me a witch."

"That explains their attack, but I still don't understand why?" asks Phoenix.

She looks at Phoenix, "You're a Chimerian; I'm not. This form you see is all that I am."

"How can that be?" queries Phoenix.

"I was told I was brought to this world many lives ago from another world; I'm not a child of this world."

"Ok, assume I believe you. Where did you come from?" asks Phoenix.

"I don't know; I was brought here by the instructor. She said I would meet my destiny here. So far, all I've found is hate and pain. Here you must be tired and hungry. Sleepover there, and I'll make up something to eat," she said.

Phoenix is tired from the long voyage by ship and the flying around the Island, so he moves over next to the wall where a mat lays on the floor. Phoenix drifts off to sleep and is awakened an hour later and given some stew to eat with water to drink.

"Thank you! Do you mind if I ask what your name is?" asked Phoenix.

The woman looked at him for a moment and then said her name is Becky, "no one had ever asked her for her name before. They just called me witch!"

"Becky, nice name; this stew is wonderful; thank you for it," said Phoenix.

"Is your name Phoenix?" asks Becky.

"Yes, it is."

"You were named for a mythical bird?" mused Becky.

"It's more than a myth. Here I've finished my stew; where may I clean up the bowl?"

"Give it to me; I'll take care of it later when it's safe to leave the cave," explains Becky.

Phoenix hands over the bowl and turns in for the night. Late in the night, Phoenix feels someone shaking him awake, and he wakes with a start. Leaning over him is a strange creature motioning him to be silent, then motions him to follow. Curious Phoenix follows the strange creature deeper into the cave. When they reach a chamber, the creature motions Phoenix to sit.

"I'm called the instructor; I'm from the hive on a different world."

"What do you want from me, Instructor?" queries Phoenix.

"When you leave this Island, you need to take Becky with you. You're her destiny that she spoke of."

"I'm what!" said Paladin.

"You heard me," said the instructor.

"I heard you; I just don't understand; how is she, my destiny?" queries Paladin.

"I brought Becky here over a thousand years ago before you were born. Her world was on the edge of dying, and she was the last of her kind. I'm from the future, so I knew when you would arrive. Becky will fill a void in your life, which your first wife Alana filled until she died of old age."

"But I hardly know Becky, and will she be willing to leave with me?" asks Phoenix.

"She will when I tell her too, she does not know you yet either, but I know your lives will be intertwined. You're destined to make her your mate for life."

"But I can't give her children; I'm a eunuch," protests Phoenix.

"That won't matter; she's so different from everyone that she can't bear children either," states the instructor.

"If you say I need to take her with me, I will, but I will not force her into anything; it must be her own choice," states Phoenix.

"I can ask no more than that," said the instructor.

The instructor leads Phoenix back to the cave where Becky sleeps; the instructor wakes Becky up and tells her Phoenix is her destiny if you want to leave this Island. Becky wants to leave the Island, so she agrees. The instructor leaves them and returns to the hive on a different world, fulfilling her mission here on this world.

"If you want to leave with me in a couple of days, you'll need to pack food and water for yourself to last four days."

"Alright, is there anything else I need to do?" asks Becky.

"I don't suppose you have heavy blanket or clothes made from leather?" asks Phoenix.

"I do. It can get very cold here, So I've made them myself."

"I have to isolate the guild masters to this island; to do that, I'll have to destroy their ships, you wait here, and I'll be back, and then we can leave the following day," says Phoenix.

Phoenix goes back to sleep, and in the morning, Becky wakes him up to give him breakfast. When Phoenix finished eating, he thanks Becky for the food and leaves the cave. So as not to attract attention, Phoenix flies off as a sparrow; when he is a mile away, he explodes into his Phoenix form and flies to the harbor, and causes such an uproar getting the attention of the men on the ships. The men fire arrows at him, but he is up too high for them to hit him. Then Phoenix burns the masts giving the men a chance to leave the ship before he sets the ships on fire, burning them down to the water before they sink to the bottom of the harbor.

Then, Phoenix flies out to sea, and once out of sight, he changes to a falcon and returns to Becky.

They returned to the cave to spend the day resting and getting ready to leave at daybreak. Phoenix prepares to make a very long trip across the ocean at day break. Just as Phoenix is about to move the stone door, he hears someone in the passage.

Phoenix turns to Becky, "Someone is in the cave." Becky grabs a wedge-shaped rock and jams it under the door to keep it from being opened. Whoever it was, started pushing on the rock to see if it would roll out of the way. The door didn't budge then it sounded like the person moved back down the cave tunnel. Phoenix decides to wait a while and see if they can leave without incident.

CHAPTER

19

Phoenix and Becky are dressed, and with her stuff packed, they move the rock and walk down the tunnel to the opening. Phoenix holds back from the entrance, then changes to a sparrow and flies out of the opening to scout the grotto and see if anyone is hiding there. Phoenix circles the grotto a couple of times but doesn't see anything. Then he drops down in front of the cave and calls Becky out. Phoenix changes to his Phoenix form, and when Becky steps out, it seems that the men come from out of nowhere as they change from rats to men and start firing arrows at them. Phoenix burns the arrows in mid-flight.

Phoenix expands his size, grabs Becky, and launches into the air, followed by more arrows. Phoenix outdistanced them and is soon out of range of the arrows. Phoenix flies to the north end of the Island then sets out for the four-day flight across the ocean with no stopovers. Phoenix flies as high as he can to avoid the headwinds, which will tire him out and make the flight longer. At the end of the fourth day, Phoenix can see the harbor city he lefts months ago. Phoenix approaches the city from the seaward side, thunders out a greeting, lands on the pier, and transforms back into his human form. He collapsed, exhausted and hungry. The regent with several men came down to greet Phoenix and soon realized there is a problem.

Becky grabs Phoenix, and she cries out to help him; the men hurry over to pick Phoenix up and carry him up to the castle and get him into a bed. "Who are you?" asked the regent.

"I'm called Becky; he flew me from the guild masters Island; he has had no food or drink for four days."

"Ok, I'll get you both some food and water. I'll have it sent to your room here. Will you be staying with him, or do you require another room?" asked the regent.

Becky says she'll stay near Phoenix. Becky, thanks to the regent for his help. Soon the food arrives, and a few flasks of water and mead come. Becky looks through the selection and finds a soup she carefully spoons into Phoenix, then lets him sleep. At the end of the second day, Phoenix wakes up and is still as hungry as a bear; he attacks his food then goes back to sleep to wake up in the morning back to his usual self.

Phoenix wakes to see Becky sitting in a chair next to his bed. Phoenix watches her for a few short minutes, gets up and dresses, lifts her gently from the chair. Then places her in his bed, and covers her. Phoenix leaves the room and goes in search of the regent and finds him holding court, so Phoenix watches to see how he does.

In the end, the regen is startled to see Phoenix watching him and smiling.

"Sire, you should've let me know you were there."

"No, my friend, it was refreshing watching you dispense your judgments. All in all, you did very well. I thank you for watching over my subjects."

"From you, Sire, that is high praise indeed. I see you've recovered; I'm glad." Looking around, "Sire, where is lady Becky?"

"I put her to bed and left her to sleep."

"I've finished my court, and I have a little time; would you care to tell me what you've been up to since you left here months ago?"

They retire to the regent's private sitting room, and Phoenix regales the regent of the coastal sea raiders of all he has done and how he met Becky. Phoenix did manage to leave out the meeting with the hive instructor.

"So! the guild masters have been stranded on their island for good then?" asked the regent.

"For now, my friend, they haven't the trees to build a ship, so they can't so easily fly here except for the sea bird people. I'd say they shouldn't be able to get to these shores for the time being."

"Excellent, Sire. Thanks for sharing." A knock at the door, "Enter," said the regent.

"Majesty, Lady Becky is awake and asking for Phoenix; she seems to be distraught."

Phoenix stands up and rushes to his apartment to find Becky crying. "Becky, what's wrong?"

"When I woke up, you were gone; I thought you…" crying, Becky looks up at Phoenix.

Phoenix walks over to Becky and pulls her close to him, "I wouldn't leave you without taking you with me."

Becky raised her tear-stained face and looked into his eyes, "You mean that?"

"Becky, our lives are tied together, and I can tell that it's true; I can no longer leave you behind than my right arm. I feel we're destined to spend the rest of our lives together."

"Are you sure?" Becky pleads.

Phoenix reaches out and pushes her auburn hair back from her face; he smiles as he touches her face brushing her tears aside. "You're so enchanting; your face reminds me of the tiger lily flower."

"What's that?" asks Becky.

"I'll show you when we reach my cottage in a far country."

There is a knock at the door, "Come in.," said Phoenix.

Two young women entered and asked if they could take Lady Becky with them.

"Why?" asks Becky, unsure she should trust anyone but Phoenix.

The older woman answered, "We thought you could use a bath and some clean clothes."

"A bath?" asks Becky.

"Go with them, Becky; you'll feel better when they finish; on second thought, I probably could use a good bath myself."

The women take Becky by the hand and lead her from the room and into another room down the hall where a hot bath awaits; they help strip Becky and help her into the water, where they pour in scented oils, and they also soap her up and give her a rub down. One of the women removes her leather clothes to clean them. Another woman enters with a couple of dresses. Waterlogged, the women help Becky from the bath. They dry her off, and Becky looks around for her Leather clothes. She is informed they were taken away to be washed and will be returned later.

"What do I wear until I get my clothes back?"

"Why my lady, you'll wear this dress." The woman holds up the frilly green gown.

"But..." started Becky.

The women giggled as they helped Becky into her dress. At first, Becky wasn't sure she wanted to wear this garment called a dress. They got Becky into the dress, combed her hair, and fitted her with some shoes. Then the woman applied the final touches to her face by using a slight blush and coloring her lips a shade of red to compliment her hair. Becky saw herself in polished sheet metal and was shocked at what she saw.

Becky was wondering how Phoenix would like what he was about to see. She was quite pretty, and she enjoyed being clean and dressed up. To her amazement, Phoenix was smiling when he saw her, and he couldn't look away from her.

Phoenix stood when she entered, and so did the regent. The regent said, "My lady Becky, you look like the lady you are!"

Phoenix took her hand and said, "The regent is right; you would put a tiger lily to shame you're so beautiful."

Becky had never been paid any compliment before, and she was unsure if they meant it or were making fun of her. She decided not to say anything but take what they said. Becky noticed that most men, including Phoenix, kept staring at her throughout the dinner. It made her feel strange and somewhat uncomfortable. At the end of the night, she admitted that being noticed was nice. She realized it was out of admiration and not hatred.

Phoenix had a bed added to his apartment for Becky as he escorted Becky back to their room. Becky enjoyed being treated like a lady; she'd never forget this day; it had been the best day of her life.

The following day the Phoenix, with Becky in tow, went to see the regent to tell him they would be moving on; Phoenix needed to return home to check on his other kingdom and take Becky with him. The regen was not happy about it, but he understood.

"Majesty, do you know when I can get my leathers back?" asked Becky.

"I have a better surprise for you, lady. If you will indulge me." The regent leads Becky and Phoenix out of the castle and to a dress shop. "Stanly, where are you?" a small man with hair sticking out in all directions. "Yes, your majesty."

"Stanly, I have lady Becky here to try on her new leather suit."

"Girls, bring out the leather outfit for lady Becky," calls Stanly.

The women bring out the leather bodysuit and cape, all decked out in plain leather but very soft compared to her makeshift suit, and the women embroidered the phoenix symbol on the front. Becky reaches out to touch the clothes, and she starts to cry. "No one has ever given her anything this nice." The shopkeeper was shocked, "Lady, what is wrong, is the suit not what you want?" says Stanly with concern in his voice.

Becky grabs the leather suit and holds on to it; between the tears, she says, "It's very nice. I love it. No one has ever given me anything so nice. Stanly, you have made me very happy. Thank you!"

Stanly sighed, "Oh my! I thought I didn't meet your expectations."

Becky walks over to Stanly, touches his face, and then plans a kiss on his forehead, and his face turns to beat red as he blushes. "My Lady, you honor me very much!"

"So, my lady Becky, do you like my gift?" asked the regent.

Becky walks over to the regent and plants a kiss on his cheek, and he clears his throat, "I'll take that as a yes," stammers the regent.

Becky took her new gift when she left to return to the castle. Becky's life here on this world has been mostly followed by pain and hatred until she met Phoenix. In the years to come, she would come to know love and caring. In the morning, she is dressed in her new leather suit and cape—the young woman who had bathed her, and gave her the new dress met her and Phoenix at the porch to tell Becky to return.

Becky promised when Phoenix returned; she would too. The women gave her a package with a new dress and some of the makeup they used on her. Becky bestowed a few hugs and kisses on them. Becky, in all her life she never experienced such kindness. Becky would treasure these moments for the rest of her long life.

With pleasantries given, Phoenix changes to his phoenix form and grabs up Becky to fly for a two-day flight to the next city-state, where Phoenix would like to see if they're still following his rule. Phoenix decides to stop at the end of the day and make camp.

Phoenix asks Becky, "would you like to have fish for dinner?"

"Whatever you bring me, I can fix it for dinner," states Becky.

Phoenix knows where the stream is, so he changes to an eagle and flies off to catch a fish. Phoenix returns with a large fish; Becky takes it, cleans it, spits it up over the fire, and cooks it. To Phoenix's surprise, it tastes delicious. Phoenix gets up and refills their water bag. That night they turn in to get some sleep. Phoenix finds Becky snuggled up next to him in the morning, sleeping soundly. Phoenix decides to go catch another fish.

Phoenix returns to see the camp packed up and ready to leave when he shows up with a nice-sized fish. Becky cooks it up, and after they eat, Phoenix changes and launches off into the air on their way to the city-state, where they'll stay the night before leaving to continue to the west coast before, they fly across the ocean for three days straight.

Phoenix touches down just outside the city, and he and Becky walk up to the gates and are admitted by the guards after Phoenix demonstrates who he is to the man guarding the entrance. The man almost came unhinged when he stopped Phoenix at the gate and refused to believe that Phoenix was who he said he was until Phoenix changed and grabbed the man and took him up very high into the air, and then the fire bolts shot down to the ground convinced the man he was the Phoenix.

Wild-eyed and not daring to open his mouth, the guard waved Phoenix and Becky through the gate. Becky started laughing when they walked a few yards into the city. Phoenix heard her laugh for the first time since he met her, it was a rich laugh, and he started laughing too.

"Was that necessary?" she giggled.

"I guess not, but his tone aggravated me, and well, you saw what I did."

"At first, I thought you would kill him; I'm so glad you didn't," she giggled.

"I suppose he won't have that tone of voice with people in the future. Let's let it drop."

When they reach the state home of the regent, Phoenix is met by the doorman. "Where's the regent? Please inform him Phoenix is here to see him."

"His majesty said not to disturb him until morning; please go along until morning."

Phoenix grabs the doorman by his shirt and pulls him close. "Go! Wake his majesty and tell him that the Phoenix is here and wants to see him!"

The doorman pulls Phoenix's hand from his shirt. "How do I know you're the Phoenix?"

"Really! Maybe that'll convince you of who I am." Phoenix changes to his Phoenix form launches up into the air, thunders out his name, and shoots down fire bolts. The doorman is on the ground on his hands and knees. "I'm sorry that I doubted you; yes, I'll go get the regent." The regent bursts out the door in an angry fit at that very moment.

"Who's making all these rucks and disturbing my sleep!" shouts the regent.

About now, Phoenix is getting angry. He fixes the regent with a look. "Regent explains yourself; I'm your king, the Phoenix."

In a mid-tirade, the regent stops to look at Phoenix, and his eyes almost pop out of his head. "Sire, I'm sorry. I didn't know you were even in the country."

"That's no excuse for treating people like I've been treated this night. I see that a change of regents may be necessary!" growls Phoenix.

"Yes, Sire, I'm at your service," fawns the regent.

"Tonight, Regent, I'll take your rooms for my lady and me. Return in the morning, and we'll see what will happen."

Phoenix escorts Becky into the house and closes the door leaving the soon to be dismissed regent standing on the front porch. The doorman followed them into the house and asked if Phoenix and his lady needed anything.

"Yes, we need some food and something to drink. Can you take care of that for us?" asked Phoenix.

"Yes, Sire, right away. Is there anything else you need?" queries the doorman.

"We could use a bath," said Becky.

"It will be ready for you shortly, along with some food. Will you bathe together or separately?" asks the doorman.

"Separately," coughed Phoenix.

"As you desire, Sire." The doorman guided them to a room with tubs for bathing, and moments later, men showed up with the hot water to fill them. Soon Phoenix and Becky are bathing, and when they finish, they find a change of clothes. Dressed and clean, they return to the dining hall to eat a meal. When they had finished their repast, they were guided to a room for sleeping. In the morning, the regent shows up and apologizes for his behavior the night before. Phoenix dismissed the man. Then told him before he and Becky leave, he would be replaced as regent.

That day Phoenix interviews the doorman and several other folks; Phoenix chooses the doorman to be the new regent, with a warning if he didn't serve the people instead of himself, he would be replaced. The doorman understood and promised to follow his rules for ruling. The next day Phoenix leaves with Becky to fly to the next town two days further.

That night during camp, Becky asks, "Do you always replace your regents with servants?"

"Not always. I try to find people who know how to serve, not be served themselves."

"Then why did you put the first regent in charge in the first place?"

"I was conquering the land; I didn't replace every leader as I went along. I gave them my rules they promised to follow; this is why I take time to visit my kingdoms to see how the people fair. If they get abused like that scum was doing, they get replaced."

"You are a fair man, Sire," said Becky.

Phoenix holds Becky by her shoulders, "Becky, you never have to call me sire; I am your servant!" Phoenix bows to her.

"You never cease to amaze me, lord Phoenix," whispers Becky.

"I hope I always keep you amazed, my lady."

Smiling, Becky hugs Phoenix and kisses him, "No one has ever cared for me like you have these few weeks we have spent together. Tomorrow will be a long day. We should get some rest; I look forward to furthering adventures with you, Phoenix."

Phoenix lays out on their bed, and they turn in to sleep; and Becky snuggles up next to Phoenix to keep warm and feel close to him. Both are falling in love, but neither wants to admit it. Phoenix was worried if he loved Becky, he would forget his dead wife, Alana. Becky was afraid she would somehow lose him.

They packed up in the morning, and continued their travel to the west. They stopped at the last town along their route to the coast. They enjoyed a couple of days with the regent and his wife, who is expecting a baby. Becky visited the woman and then came to Phoenix, "the poor woman will lose her baby; she is very sick." Becky broke down and started to cry.

Phoenix is very touched by Becky's caring, so he hands Becky a vile of his tears. "Becky, go give this vile to the woman to drink, and she'll be healed."

"What will this do?" Becky asked.

"I'm a Phoenix in every sense; my tears will heal her from her sickness."

Becky takes the vile to the regent's wife and mixes the tears with some water. "Here, your majesty, drink this all down every drop. The regent's wife looks at Becky. Are you sure her look seems to ask? Becky assures her it'll be alright. The woman drinks down the water, and within a few long minutes, her color changes from a pale parlor to a vibrantly healthy look, and she seems to gain her strength enough to get up and walk around.

"What did you give me to drink?" asks the regent's wife.

Becky smiled, "the tears of the Phoenix heal," said Becky.

The regent's wife gets dressed, and with Becky at her side, they walk to the sitting room. The wife summons her husband. Her husband came into her sitting room, "Wife, why are you out of bed?

He was stunned; his wife was in the very pink of health. The husband kneels beside his wife, takes her hand, and quietly cries because of this miracle; the leeches said she would die in childbirth and the child may die. Phoenix places a hand on the kneeling regent and helps him up, and guides him from the room.

"Here, my friend, Phoenix hands the regent a couple of vials; these are my tears. They'll heal anyone as long as they still have a spark of life. Becky gave them to your wife, and now she and the child are healthy."

"Thank you, Sire! Whatever I can do, let me know."

"Kelly, you are doing what I want. You are serving my people; keep it up."

"I will with all my heart, Sire."

Becky came to Phoenix, "I want to stay for another week; the baby is about to be born; I want to be here."

"I guess we don't need to be anywhere anytime soon; we can stay for the baby."

Becky squeals with delight and hugs Phoenix's neck. "Thank you, my lord!"

It took two weeks for the baby to arrive, so during that time, Phoenix located a smithy and got permission to use the smithy's tools and forge. Phoenix forges out a couple of medallions, one for Becky and one for the baby (knowing the baby wouldn't get it until it was older).

The day came, and Phoenix and the regent were told to go do something and leave this to the women. Ejected, the men went on a walk to visit a few people; the regent's mind is not on what they are doing. He was thinking of his wife and child. Two hours later, they returned to the home to find a flurry of women running about and in a hurry. The two men went to the throne room and paced back and forth, waiting on the child's birth.

Several hours later, an older woman came out to the throne room with a bundle; it was a little girl. The woman pulled down the cover to reveal her tiny face, and the regent was trembling as he touched that little hand; concerned, he asked, "How is my wife?"

"She is doing well and is asleep your majesty."

"May I see her?"

"Yes, go see her."

Phoenix walks up to the old woman, "May I see her?"

"Oh, yes, Sire."

The old woman holds up the baby and uncovers her. Phoenix touches the baby's hand and smiles. "She is such a precious little bundle of joy."

The regent finds his wife sleeping, and she has a smile on her face; he reaches down and takes her hand, and she wakes up and hugs him. "Did you see your daughter?"

"I sure did, and she is as beautiful as you are."

"Lier, I look a fright."

"No, my love, you never looked more beautiful than now."

The old woman placed the child in her mother's arms—the regent hugged his wife and daughter. Phoenix walks into the room and sees Becky watching the regent. Phoenix gives Becky a small necklace to give to the regent for the baby. Becky looks at the medallion and sees it's shaped like a Phoenix. Becky looks to and thanks Phoenix for the baby gift. Becky presents it to the regent as a gift. They thank

Becky. Phoenix and Becky bid them farewell two days later and flew off to the west.

Phoenix flies straight through to the west coast and lands beside the mouth of the river where he encountered Fang's men several years ago. They set up camp, and Phoenix changes to an eagle and flies up the stream to find a fat fish for dinner. Phoenix swoops down and snags the fish, and starts to fly back to the camp when he hears in his mind that he needs to land. Phoenix lands and changes to his human form, and from out of thin air, the hive instructor steps out into the open.

"Hail Phoenix King of this world."

"Why did you contact me, instructor?"

"To give you information about this world."

"What information might that be?"

"A history, if you will, and then a warning."

"All right, I'm listening."

"This world was a thriving world. The guild masters populated it; they originally owned this world. But greed and wars followed by plagues killed them, except those who moved to that Island you exiled them to."

"I thought they were Chimerians."

"No, they can change their shape, but they can only assume the shape of a rat or a raven. They tried to mate with your kind and found it wouldn't work. They couldn't produce any offspring. So, they tried to come back after the sea raiders found their Island. Now you see what they are now, a dying race."

"Then am I to blame for their demise?"

"No, they caused their downfall. This history was something you should know. Now Becky is also not of this world."

"If you recall, you already told me this already."

"Oh, that was not me; it was another instructor."

"Another instructor?"

"We are from another world and also from the future. That's how I knew where and when to find you."

"Ok, is there anything else I need to know?"

"Yes, don't be afraid to make Becky your wife; you won't forget Alana, she'll always be in your heart, but you have the capacity to love another. Becky will live as long as you live."

"I do care deeply for her," said Phoenix.

"Then you need to overcome her fear of you possibly leaving her. Becky will be in grave danger in your next life span, and you'll need to protect her."

"Protect her from what?"

"I'm not allowed to tell you, but I'm allowed to give you the warning, and I have. Now I must return to my world. Farewell, King Phoenix."

The instructor disappears, leaving Phoenix perplexed. Then he changes back to the eagle and returns to camp with the fish.

"What's wrong, Phoenix?" asks Becky.

"I just had an encounter with the hive instructor."

"What did you talk about?"

"The history of this world."

"Anything else?"

"She said I need to make you, my wife."

"Your wife!?"

Phoenix reaches into his pocket, pulls out another necklace, and hands it over to Becky. "Would you be my wife?"

Becky looks over the necklace, "Did you make this, or did you buy it?"

"I'll have you know I'm an excellent craftsman; I made it. Do you like it?"

"Yes, I do like it. Do you want me to wife, or are you doing this because of the instructor?"

"Both; the instructor said I'd not forget my first wife if I married you and that I would not suffer the loss of you as I did my Alana."

"You miss her, don't you?" asks Becky.

"Yes, there's not a day that I don't think of her. Having you with me helps to divert my heart and mind."

Becky walks over to Phoenix, hugs him, and whispers, "I'd be honored to be your wife." Becky leans down and kisses the top of Phoenix's forehead.

Becky turned away and set about to cook the fish. The following day, they break camp and grab some hardtack for breakfast; for the next three days, they'd be flying over the open ocean, with no place to land. Phoenix changes to his phoenix shape and scoops up Becky, and flies for the next three days until they hit the east coast of New-Land. Rather than landing, Phoenix flies on for most of the day and lands at his cottage.

CHAPTER

20

"Becky, we're now at my home away from home. We'll make the rounds of this kingdom in a few days, and you'll get to meet some of my family."

Phoenix takes her into the cottage and sees that the caretaker has been keeping the place up for him. There is no food here, so Phoenix decides to get something to eat after some rest and a little more hardtack. Hours later Phoenix flies down into the valley and locates a deer-like animal. He pounces on it, breaks its neck, then flies back in his talons and drops it off next to the skinning rack.

Becky comes out to see what Phoenix brought home. "Wow, I've never seen any animal like this. What is it?" Becky asks.

"Someone in the past called it a deer. It's good meat; if you like, I can show you how to skin and clean it," said Phoenix.

Becky takes off her cloak and helps hoist the deer onto a rack and stretch it out. Phoenix guts it and separates the organs that are good to eat. Phoenix covers the deer to leave it for the next day so it would cool off to make it easy to skin and cut up. That morning they had heart for breakfast and lunch. For dinner, they ate liver.

Phoenix shows Becky how to skin the deer-like creature and then puts the skin on a stretching rack to begin tanning the hide. Phoenix cuts up the animal and takes part of it to the kitchen. The rest he puts into the smokehouse and smokes the meat to preserve it.

Becky stays in his mother's room and has or can wear any dress in the closet. Becky dresses up and comes to dinner; Phoenix decides to change his clothes and takes a cold bath. Phoenix makes one of his mother's stews. He had collected some wild vegetables from his garden to add to the stew.

Becky liked what he had made. Later that evening, "Becky, do you know how to dance?"

"What is that?" she asks.

"Fair enough. Would you like me to teach you?"

"Ok, when?"

"Right now."

Phoenix takes Becky's hand and leads her to the middle of the room and starts with basic steps, and he hums a tune as they dance. Becky is shocked at how easy she can follow along with his steps. She is also confused at how close they had to be when they danced. It made her blush. Phoenix leans down and kisses her.

Later that evening, Phoenix was reading a book, and Becky asked, "what was he doing?"

"I'm reading the words in this book."

Becky moves up next to him and looks at the pages; to her, they are just a bunch of gibberish or spidery script. "I don't understand?" she exclaims.

"You don't know how to read?" asks Phoenix.

"No, what is reading?"

Phoenix closes his book and walks to a cupboard, and takes down some paper and an inkwell with a quill. "Becky, come sit here next to me."

Becky sits down next to Phoenix. Phoenix starts with the alphabet, and he writes each letter and names it. Then he has her do the same. Then over a few days, they progressed to words, sentences, paragraphs. Then Phoenix had Becky read to him. It was awkward at first, then she caught on more and more and was soon reading fluently.

Phoenix moves on to numbers, and she becomes proficient in a few months. The dance lessons became fencing lessons. With time she becomes adept at swordplay. One day Kimi showed up to check on the cottage only to find Becky at the house.

"Who are you!" asks Kimi, "this is my uncle's home. You don't belong here!"

"I'm Becky; Phoenix is off hunting. He'll be back soon."

"Ok, I'll wait with you if you lied to me…" Kimi did not finish her statement, but she conveyed her intent.

"Now that you know my name, what is yours?" asked Becky.

"Not that means anything; I'm called Kimi."

"Kimi, would you like some tea while we wait?"

Kimi thought it over and said, "Alright."

Becky led the way into the house. Becky let Kimi make the tea because Kimi didn't trust Becky yet. Soon they are both talking when Kimi sees the necklace Becky is wearing.

"Is something wrong, Kimi?"

"Who made that necklace?"

"Phoenix did; he gave it to me when he asked me to marry him."

"May I see it?" asks Kimi.

Becky took off the necklace and handed it to Kimi. Kimi inspected it closely, "You say my uncle made this."

"Yes. Is something wrong?"

"No, it is his work; I would recognize it anywhere."

"I'm glad you are sure of me. I find that I have a powerful feeling for your uncle."

"Do you love him?" asked Kimi.

"I don't know. I know that I feel pain in my heart when he's not near me. And he makes me feel like I'm the only one who is important to him. I know of Alana, and I wished I could know more about her."

"The only person alive that can tell you that is my uncle, but I think he'll color the story very lovingly. My Aunt was a vicious killer when it was necessary to protect her own. She killed her father for killing her only child. She ripped out a man's throat for threatening to kill her adopted daughter. You see, Alana was a wolf in her other guise."

"Thanks for the information. Kimi, what is a tiger lily flower?"

"Come with me. Did Phoenix compare you to that flower?"

"Why yes," said Becky

"I'm not surprised." Kimi led Becky from the house and walked down the road, and at the edge of the woods, there were a lot of Tiger lily flowers.

"What pretty flowers!" exclaimed Becky.

"See the freckles, Becky?"

Laughing, "Yes, they are pretty, and the freckles a lot like mine." Becky knelt to pick them.

"See why he compared them to you or you to them?"

"I do. Does he see me that way?"

"Becky, my uncle does not toy with people, and if he told you, you are that pretty, he meant it. My uncle is one of a kind. Suppose he has chosen you for a mate. He means it."

Becky hugs Kimi. "Thank you for being kind."

"Becky, please tell me about yourself,"

"Where to start to start. First, Kimi, how old do you think I am?"

"A little older than me, one hundred years, why?"

"I'm two thousand years old, I'm even older than your uncle, and will live for thousands of years into the future. I'm from a different world. The Hive instructor brought me from my world and left me here. I suffered many things at the hands of the guild masters and sea raiders. I was branded a witch, so I hid in the wilderness."

"How did my uncle find you?"

"Several months ago, your uncle heard me screaming for my life, and he stopped the two men who were about to kill me, he killed one of the guild masters, and the other got a way to go bring others to track me down. I led your uncle to my hidden cave, and we stayed there until he brought me off the island to the sea raiders' country. Eventually, we traveled here."

"We best get back; I need to talk to my uncle and bring him up to date on what has happened since he has been gone."

The women hurry back to the cottage; Phoenix drops out of the sky in his eagle form as they arrive. "Becky, I was worried you weren't at home; I see you met my great-grandniece; I hope you were getting along."

"Not, at first, uncle, but she convinced me she was with you; I showed her a tiger lily flower."

"I see."

They return to the cottage, and Kimi talks about the plague. Some of the other things like Mara and Orion and the new building to grow some of the plants from the jungle, Mara even now shows people how to use them, and she also has Fenwick's book duplicated by the scribes for others to have.

After Kimi finished, Phoenix regales her of his conquest of the sea raiders county. And how he exiled the guild masters to an island, and he glosses over the story of Becky.

"I need to visit my kingdom to let everyone know I'm back, and I also need to see the historian at castle Phoenix and tell him of my adventures."

"When will you be going, uncle? If it is ok, I'd like to hitch a ride so I can visit Mara!"

"Tomorrow morning, ok, with you gals."

"I'll be here early in the morning, uncle." Kimi steps out into the yard, changes into a raven, and flies toward home.

"Your niece is very nice but protective of her uncle."

"She is that. Now come and let me show you how to clean and dress a grouse."

"When will you marry me, Phoenix?"

"When would you like to get married?"

"I'm ready to be your wife."

"I tell you what, how about we get married within the week, we'll be at castle Phoenix, and I'm sure Kimi and Mara will want to make a big event out of it."

"Alright!"

Kimi is there waiting for them to get up and be off in the morning. Kimi made breakfast. When Phoenix and Becky got up, they sat down to cold fish and veggies. Then they all cleaned up the cottage. They moved out into the yard. Phoenix changes to his Phoenix form and scoops up both women, and flies off to the castle; they arrive around noon in time for lunch.

Phoenix screamed out in his booming voice to let everyone know he was back; as he touched down in the courtyard, a crowd gathered, and they cheered his return. Ted, the regent, is waiting at the top of the stairs with Orion. They greeted Phoenix and his passengers.

"Well, met King Phoenix," shouts Ted.

Phoenix grasps Ted's hand in a warm handshake, "It's nice to be home, my friend; how has the kingdom faired with my being gone?"

"Let us get inside and away from all the cheering, and I'll tell you all that has happened," shouts Ted.

Phoenix leads them into the castle and heads for the dining room, where they can get some cold mead and relax. Before he regales his audience with his conquest of the sea raiders and how he'll have to spend time with them and this kingdom, he tells them about Becky and how they met.

Ted and Orion talk about the plague and all they did to stop it. How if it weren't for Mara, they might all be dead.

"Speaking of Mara, where is she," asked Phoenix.

As if by magic Mara appears and rushes over to Phoenix to hug him, Becky is standing by Phoenix, and Orion shouts "No!" and grabs Becky and pulls her away from Phoenix. Everyone, including Mara, forgets how poisonous her touch can be. Orion's quick thinking may have saved Becky from dying.

"Oh my, I forgot that not everyone is protected from my poison."

Orion let's Becky go then pulls her to one side. "My Mara is a poison dart person, and her touch can kill in seconds; I'm sorry if I hurt you, my lady," said Orion.

Mara finished hugging Phoenix, then she left the room and ran to her apartment and moments later returned and hands Becky a vial with the antidote to her poison. Mara encourages Becky to drink it down. Becky looks to Phoenix, and he indicates that she should drink it down. Becky drinks the potion, and Mara takes her hand. "It's nice to meet you," said Mara.

Phoenix gets up. It's nearing evening, and before he goes off to bed, he wants to make an appointment with the historian to spend a few days with him to get what has happened down on paper. As an afterthought, Phoenix announces his desire to marry Becky. Phoenix hears the girls giggle and carry on from where Mara and Kimi sit. As Phoenix leaves, the girls gather up Becky and fuss over her. Phoenix realizes the girls will make a big production from the wedding and smiles.

CHAPTER

21

Becky is not used to being the center of attention and is uncomfortable, but she also finds it pleasant. Becky has been in hiding and abused; now, people are caring for her. They are making a big deal over her. She is not used to that. That night in Phoenix's apartment, Becky starts crying, causing Phoenix to gather her up into his arms and ask her what was wrong.

Becky looks into his face, "I'm happy, and I can't stop crying."

"Becky, everything will be ok, I promise. Once we're married, all the hoopla will end."

"I've never had anyone who cares about me, and now everyone wants to be my friend."

"It's bed time now Becky, you sleep on the bed. I had a camp bed brought in for me. Tomorrow the girls will take you out, and you'll get what they call (some girl time). I just thought I would warn you."

"Will that be alright with you, Phoenix?"

"It'll be fine; besides, Orion and Ted want to show me Mara's greenhouse, and I suspect they'll ask me permission to wed a couple of girls."

That night Becky had a hard time sleeping; not sure of what girl time was, she wasn't sure if she'd like it. The next day the girls dress up Becky, and they all head to Mara's apartment to talk about the wedding, what they should wear. Then the ball afterward. It didn't take long, and Becky began to enjoy it.

Phoenix is led to the smithy, where they're going to tour Mara's greenhouse and see what she had the scribes doing copying Fenwick's book. They show Phoenix how they set up a relay to the south in case of more problems like they had with this plague. Phoenix ooh's and aah's the whole works.

"Alright, guys, why are we here? I suspect there is more going on here than a tour," said Phoenix.

Both men stand looking down at the ground, unsure how to ask Phoenix about the women. Orion wants to marry Mara, and Ted wants permission to ask Kimi for a wife.

Phoenix starts laughing, "You guys are so transparent; tell me what you want to ask me."

"I want permission to marry Mara," stammers Orion.

"I want to marry Kimi," blurts Ted.

"You have my permission, as long as the girls agree. I'll leave you men to gather your courage to ask them. Don't wait too long, or they may turn you down for taking too long."

Orion walks toward where the women are planning for Becky's wedding. Ted follows Orion. Orion couldn't wait to ask Mara; Ted, on the other hand, was pale and unsure. Phoenix stands back and watches both men with a chuckle just under his breath. Phoenix is sure of what Mara would say, but Kimi is more complex. She likes being on her own.

Orion asks Mara and receives a long yes with her kiss and hug. Ted stands before Kimi and stammers that he loves her and would like to have her as a wife. You could see the wheels in her head as she mauled it over, and to Phoenix's surprise, she said yes. Ted nearly faints, and Kimi stands up to hold him up to keep him from falling. After Ted recovers, Phoenix watches the wheels clicking in Kimi's head. She went into a huddle with Becky and Mara.

The girls told their men we wanted to get married on the same day as Becky.

"That is only a few days away; we don't have time," exclaims Orion and Ted.

The girls rush the men out of the room, and the women double down on the planning. We'll use the dresses we already have, and we'll be ready for the wedding day. Kimi turned to the men, "go get your wedding clothes, now get out of here!" said the women.

Orion and Ted go to the tailor shop to get fitted and pay for the short time they have to make them. Phoenix still had his original wedding outfit, he pulled it out of the closet, and tried it on. Phoenix finds it a bit snug, so he takes it to the tailor to have his outfit let out to fit.

On the wedding day, the men are decked out in their finery. Phoenix was in a deep blue doublet and brown hose with a cape and his sword strapped to his waist. Orion was all in black trimmed in silver; he, too, carried a sword. Ted was decked out in a deep green doublet and brown hose. He didn't have a sword, so he wore his crown of office, then he added a knife to his belt to finish off his outfit.

The woman wore beautiful gowns with all the frills; all the dresses were blue trimmed in silver, Becky's dress had a Trane, and it dragged as she walked, and she was flanked on either side by Kimi and Mara. They approached the men, and the men stepped out to take his future bride, then positioned themselves in front of the senior scribe who pronounced the wedding ceremony at the end, the men kiss the brides, and the crowed started cheering.

After the wedding, there is a grand ball, where they all dance until late into the night. The wedding couple leaves the ball early; Ted takes Kimi to his small home away from the castle where they can be alone, Orion and Mara go to the smithy. Phoenix and Becky go to their apartment for the night. In the morning, the wedding couples met up for breakfast.

Mara and Kimi have smug smiles like the cat who got into the cream, while their men have expressions of amazement. Becky is not only amazed but somewhat in wonder. Phoenix is just happy. Phoenix realizes the instructor was right. He'd never forget Alana, but Becky would fill the empty void in his life.

Phoenix and his wife Becky tour his present kingdom. It takes a year. In the end, Phoenix flies to the east coast of New-Land to search for a place where he can build a new city with a deep-water cove to start trade with the sea raiders. Phoenix would leave the castle in a day to make a round trip of his kingdom to show off Becky and let everyone know he was back. This would be a way to unite both kingdoms and open up communications between them so he wouldn't have to travel so much from one country to another.

It took a couple of months, and Phoenix found the spot that would work. As luck would have it, there was a small fishing village already there; this would help make it a hub for trading and grow it into a city. Phoenix flies back to castle Phoenix and then puts out the word to the communication hub that he is looking for people to help build a new city on the east coast to trade with the sea raiders. This message flowed out to the southern kingdom and all the other regents. Within the month, a great wave of people and families started flowing to the east to be part of the building of a new city and to get in on the new trading center.

These were primarily people looking to get a new property and start their own business. Or people who wouldn't inherit property because of their older siblings. This was a chance for them to carve out their fortunes. Pheonix and his wife Becky met them and led them to the new land to begin building. Phoenix gave them time to develop their own homes for their families; then, he pulled together knowledgeable people to see how to build the docks for loading and loading ships.

This became discouraging. No one knew how even to begin to build any docks. At the first attempt, the dock fell into the sea. Perplexed, Phoenix was brooding about it when Becky gave him an idea.

"Dear, why not go to the sea raiders and get help? They've built ships and docks. Why could they not be used here?" asks Becky.

"You realize I'll have to leave you behind to do what you suggest."

"I know. Will you take me home to our cottage before you leave?"

"I will," said Phoenix.

Chapter

22

Phoenix calls together the leaders who were a part of the new city and tells them what he has in mind to do. They all agreed this would be better than wasting man-hours and materials. After all, we're going to welcome them with trade, and they could build new ships as well. Phoenix takes Becky home so he would be able to bring more people back with him and also gets the sea raiders to build more ships for commerce and not for war.

Phoenix launches early in the morning to cross the ocean to the sea raiders' country. Phoenix enlisted his people there to start trade with his home country New-Land. During his flight, Phoenix decides to have the people of each continent come up with new cities along the coast. Before Phoenix realizes it, he lands next to the stream where this adventure started. Phoenix flew on to Fang's village to get some rest and food.

Phoenix is welcomed with open arms. Phoenix tells Fang why he's here. Fang is very interested. His village would benefit from the trade. Fang could build a small trading hub just down the coast from where he is now located. Fang suggests that Phoenix fly to the city on the east coast to get some engineers to build your docks. And I'll let the other cities and towns know of the trade possibilities. Then we can start building ships again.

Thanks, Fang; I'll leave in the morning; when can you send runners or fliers to pass the word? I already have Sire. I have my people ready to clear the cove I have in mind. This is great, Sire. Things were getting stagnant here; this will pump new life into our country.

In the early morning, Phoenix bids farewell to Fang and flies to the east to seek out these people called engineers. It takes a month to reach the east coast city and wait for the word to get out about the need for engineers. Before he knew it, Phoenix had twenty engineers ready to go to his kingdom, called New-Land. Phoenix can't carry all the engineers, so he asks for engineers who can build docks and other necessary structures for loading and unloading ships. The raiders call their land Randal after one of the founders.

The other engineers would be welcome, but they would need to come by ship when they have them built. Phoenix told them that they needed to travel to the west coast and meet up with Fang and his people; they would need engineers to help them build a new city with a port.

This started an exodus to the west coast. The thought of trade and the possibility of plying their trade in another land appeals to the sea raiders. Phoenix flew six engineers to the west coast of Randal, and he needed to rest before the crossing of the ocean to New-land. The engineers make themselves ready for the three-day trip across the ocean. On the second day, Phoenix said he was ready, and they would be leaving that morning. Phoenix changes into his Phoenix form, scoops up the men, and sets out over the ocean. Three days later, he arrives on the east coast of New-Land near the new city, where he drops off the engineers.

Phoenix spent the day in the new city to get his strength back from the long flight. Phoenix introduces the engineers to the city leaders, and they are to take the lead in building the docks and the ships. The people were ready, and they worked well with the engineers. Phoenix was satisfied with the progress and then flew home to his wife, Becky.

Phoenix flies' home, and as he comes in for a landing, Becky waits in the yard for him. Phoenix asks, "how did she know he was home."

"I don't know; I felt you were near, so I stepped out into the yard, and you were here."

"It feels good to be home," says Phoenix.

"How goes your project, dear," asks Becky.

"Actually, better than I thought it would. We're at the beginning of world peace, and we're at the beginning of world trade. In time each land will decide what to trade," says Phoenix.

True to his word, this world found peace between New-land and Randal under Phoenix's rule. The few tyrants who tried to usurp

Phoenix's rule found the people not only resistant but hostile. A few usurps barely got away with their lives. The two lands exchanged people and ideas. Over time Phoenix found himself less and less needed. In time Phoenix and Becky faded from sight.

With each generation, Mara's toxic poison became less and less until they were no longer toxic. Mara and Orion had a few children. The children are still toxic, but not as toxic as a mom.

Kimi and Ted also have several children, and one of the male children took over Kimi's house and eventually married and had children. From time to time, they'd visit Todd (Phoenix) and Becky, or they'd keep Todd's house as Todd and Becky traveled the world.

Three hundred years have passed, and everyone who was alive when peace between the lands Randal and New-Land have died off. Leaving the new generation to assume it had always been this way. Phoenix and Becky spent a lot of time traveling, and on such a trip, they located an island off the southwest coast of New-Land in the tropics, but no one lived there. Over time Phoenix builds a cabin, and they would stay there. On occasion, Phoenix would covertly visit the new history scribes and make the scribe swear not to say anything. Phoenix would dictate all that has happened. Then he'd leave with Becky and live the quiet life either on the Island or sometimes back in the valley where Phoenix and Alana had lived.

At the end of nine hundred years, Phoenix would fly back to the mountain where he buried Alana and build a funeral Pryor to get ready to set it on fire. Phoenix was getting old, and Becky still looked like her beautiful self when he met her. Phoenix left Becky at the cottage that had a clear view of the mountain.

"Becky, it's time; I must die and be reborn. I'm leaving you here if I don't come back you can live out your life here. If all goes as before, I should be back in three days."

Becky kisses Phoenix as if she may never see him again. Phoenix flies off to the mountain. Phoenix lies on the woodpile and, using his power; he sets the wood and himself on fire. The flames are so bright that Becky can see them from the cottage. Becky watches until the fires die out. She returns to the cottage to wait. On the third day, Phoenix bursts forth in his new shape of the Phoenix in black and white with blue flame surrounding him.

Phoenix lets out a scream that is heard all up and down the valley from the mountain top. Becky runs out into the yard and watches her Phoenix as he flies her way. The new Phoenix lands in the front yard in his new Phoenix form. He is black and white with an aurora of blue flame surrounding him. After a few moments, Phoenix changes to his human form and stands there in his new body, and he is young again. He stands there trying to recall who he is for a few moments.

"Phoenix, you've returned to me," cried Becky.

Phoenix stares at her. It takes a few moments, and his memories come flooding back. "Becky?" he asks.

"Yes, it's me, Becky, your wife."

Becky leaps into his arms; she is afraid he might forget her; Phoenix holds her in his strong arms. "Yes, Becky, I remember!" Phoenix lets her go and looks at his body, and sees he has regenerated. "This looks different than I looked a few days ago. Do you approve?"

Becky starts laughing and crying at the same time. "Oh, yes!" said Becky.

"I suppose we'll need to make the rounds to all the kingdoms to let them know I still live."

"Why, these last three hundred years, you have let the kingdoms alone and not shown up. You've become a wonder to the people. You're becoming a myth; they know you united the lands and brought peace and freedom. Beyond that, they are beginning to think you've gone into history," says Becky.

"They don't need to know I'm still around, do they?" asks Phoenix.

"Why? you have the people so well entrenched in the freedom that they no longer need you to interfere in their lives anymore. That doesn't mean we can't travel the kingdoms to see how they're doing without revealing who we are," suggested Becky.

"I like that idea very much. In time they'll forget the Phoenix and govern themselves, and you and I can live our own lives," ponders Phoenix.

Hugging Phoenix, Becky agrees, "it would be nice to have you all to myself."

Chapter 23

On the island of the guild masters, they're dying out, and only a few still live there. The danger the Hive instructor had warned Phoenix about is happening. A shimmering in the air occurs on the island, and fifty creatures' step from their world (dimension) into Phoenix's world. They're searching for Becky, the last princess of her world, and they want her dead! The men looked like beetles shaped like men. They're as tall as men, and they walk upright. Their upper arms have claws that can rend a man in half.

They can't talk like us. They use clicks and whistles to communicate with one another. One other thing they can use their antenna to touch a person and drain their victim's mind of all thought; of course, it kills the person. The beetle men conquered Becky's world and have killed all her people. Becky had been sent to this world to protect her and give her a chance to live.

The beetle men don't want to let her live; all they understand is destruction and killing. They have done that on several other worlds;

after they kill the princess, they'll bring their people here to this world to destroy it as well. The beetle men looked alike except for the leader; he had two great white spots on his back. (We will refer to him as white spot).

The beetle men are very hard to kill. The guild masters find that out the hard way. The guild masters attack the beetle men using spears and arrows, only to watch the weapons bounce off the hard armor of the beetles. One of the guild masters tried using a sword on white spot only to be captured. The Beetles spread out to search the island and find Becky's spore all over the island. They even find the cave where she spent most of her time here on this island.

White spot uses his antenna to drain the guild master's mind and doesn't find the answer white spot is looking for. According to the guild master, the witch lived here, but she disappeared a thousand years ago from the island. Hungry white spot eats the guild master bones and all. The other beetle men follow suit and drain everyone's mind; they eat the remaining people. The beetle men mill about the island trying to find the princess's spore or herself. They find nothing more, so they wait until morning to see where the sun comes up, and they'll head in that direction to begin the search for the princess.

The guild masters are now all dead. They will not try to reclaim the world as they once had in times past. Now the beetle men will set out to destroy another world in their task to kill the last princess of their former world. In the morning, the beetle men see where the sun comes up, and they launch off into the air and fly in the direction of the rising sun.

This will put them on the west coast of New-Land. The way to New-Land will take them a couple of weeks to fly there. As they fly in that direction, they get tired. On the third day out, they hover over the water, and the white spot has one of the beetles' land, and nothing happens. As the white spot is about to land with the rest of the beetle men, a large fish swims up and sucks the loan beetle into its mouth and swims away.

White spot and his men decide to fly on until another beetle falls out of the sky onto the ocean, where another large fish eats the lone beetle. White spot realizes they have to rest, so he decides to have them all settle on the water as one and lock their legs together to seem that they are too big to eat. This seems to work. They drift along on the water until sunrise. When they launch up out of the water and head for the eastern horizon.

Over the two weeks, they come in sight of the west coast of New-Land, where they are seen by the coast watchers Phoenix had placed there six hundred years ago. They light the signal fires to warn the other watchers and send word to the nearby settlements and on to the communication center. The communication center will notify castle Phoenix and the southern kingdom of the threat.

The powers that be will mobilize the armies to fight the threat and gather the people to safety in a few days. The whole of New-land kingdom is standing together to face the unknown danger. Of course, there's always someone who believes they can remain hidden or stand against the enemy by themselves. In this case, the beetle men find a large homestead, and the men show a brave front, then soon find they can't stand up against the beetle men. The battle is relatively short as the beetles kill and consume the ten men who stand against them. White spot directs the remaining forty-eight to follow him in the eastward direction.

In a week, the beetles reach the communication center of New-Land, and they find it empty as the word is carried to castle Phoenix and the southern kingdoms of the invasion of strange creatures. At the communication center white spot detects the princess's spoor. It proves that she has been here before at least a few times; one direction shows she has traveled to the east and south from this place.

White spot takes thirty of his army with him and sends the balance to the south to search for their prey. White spot heads to castle Phoenix in search of his quarry; then, they'll contact the queen in the other world to come through the portal to take over this world. In three weeks, white spot and his army get to castle Phoenix and notes the princess's spoor is strong here. Not fearing much by way of opposition, they approach the castle.

As the beetle's approach, a curtain of arrows from the castle walls meets them head-on. Six beetle men fall from the sky, pierced through by arrows tipped with the starstone metal. Some of the men have swords and spears made from starstone. The beetles don't figure out that some of the defending armies of men have star-metal which they find can hurt them.

The news spreads that strange creatures that looked like giant beetles are attacking New-Land at castle Phoenix. It doesn't take long for the beetles to realize they can be repelled and killed by these primitive people and their crude weapons. At the encounter of the beetle men, a messenger has reached Todd's (Phoenix) cottage. The messenger movies on to warn others.

"No!" cries, Becky. "They can't be here!"

"Who?" asks Todd.

"The very creatures who killed everyone in my world. I barely escaped with my life, and they must have found the portal I used. We must stop them, or they'll overrun this world and strip it of all life as they did on my world," cries Becky.

The battle back at castle Phoenix continues, and the people with starstone weapons manage to hold back the beetle warriors. Sadly, several people were killed who didn't have starstone weapons. One man with a sword managed to cut off the antenna of one beetle man, and it became ineffective in the fight, so more men started removing the antenna of other beetles. It makes it easy to kill the beetle men. White spot pulls his dwindling army back from the city and heads west in retreat. He has only fifteen men left, so he calls back the beetle men who went south.

The beetle army retreats to the west coast to wait for the beetle men from the south to return. They'll have to return to the portal to gather more armies. Phoenix flies to castle Phoenix, but he lands with Becky on its outskirts, and they walk into the castle courtyard.

Todd visited the scribe who knew who he was to get what's happened. Phoenix finds out that the beetle men were driven off and retreated to the west.

The scribe passed on the information about killing the beetles with starstone weapons; The writer also told Todd about cutting off the antenna of the beetles. Todd talks to Becky, and she confirms that the antenna is the only way they can perceive the world around them. It seems to make them blind and easy to approach to kill.

"Phoenix, you have to stop them. They'll return to the portal and bring through thousands, and they will overrun your world!" pleads Becky.

"Then I must stop them! That means I have to leave you here, Becky; to cross the ocean to the west to the island is a five-day non-stop flight. I can't carry you without food and water for that long," states Phoenix.

"I'll stay here, is there somewhere or someone I can stay with?" asks Becky.

"I'll have the scribe take care of you until I return," said Phoenix.

"I'd be honored, Sire, to keep her safe," says the scribe.

"Good, that's settled, Becky. I'll return as soon as I can." Phoenix kissed and hugged his wife, Phoenix ran down the castle's steps into the courtyard, then launched up into the air as the Phoenix. Roaring out to let the people know he is still around and going to protect them from the beetle men.

Phoenix knew he didn't know where the portal was except for the island, so instead of killing them before they returned to the portal, he'd have to restrain himself from destroying them before he could find the portal. Phoenix flies to the west coast at a very high altitude, and he passes the beetle army as they travel west. Phoenix flies onto the coast to wait for them to show.

Phoenix reaches the last homestead or ranch before the coast; he finds it empty; the blood and the bones tell the story. It'd take the beetles a week to reach the coast where he is waiting. Phoenix will fly high to see if he can watch them make sure they're coming this way. Phoenix goes to the barn to create a place to stay when he hears what sounds like children playing.

CHAPTER 24

Phoenix follows the noise and finds the house where the women and children had holed up when the beetles first came to their ranch, and the men went out to defend their home. As he stands there seeing them, one of the women moves up behind Phoenix with a heavy pan and lays him out flat before she realizes that he's no threat. An hour later, one of the women threw water on the Phoenix, and he came spluttering awake.

"What happened?" demands Phoenix.

"I hit you with a frying pan; I'm sorry, I thought you were one of the beetle men, and I was protecting everyone," she stated meekly.

He was rubbing his head with an "Ouch! It's ok, I can understand. The beetle men are headed back here. That's why I'm here. I have to follow them and stop them," said Phoenix.

"How do you intend to stop them when our men couldn't?" asks the headwoman.

"I'm the Phoenix."

"Your who?" gasped the woman in surprise."

"I'm the Phoenix, and I can stop them."

"I hit the king? Oh, my, I'm so sorry!" she exclaimed.

Laughing, Phoenix said, "you're a formidable woman. Then being serious, when I tell you to hide, you must hide the children and the women and be very quiet."

"We understand, and we'll do as you say."

"Very well, would it be alright if I shared your food?" asked Phoenix.

"We'd be glad to, but all our livestock is scared off, and we don't have anything but what's in the root cellar."

"Give me a moment, and I'll hunt up some large game for you," said Phoenix.

Phoenix launches into the air and heads north; within the hour, he finds a heard of deer, and he brings down two of them and carries them back to the ranch where the women and children take the animals and dress them out, and that night, they have a feast of deer and what vegetables they have in the root cellar. Everyone goes to bed that night with a full belly.

In the morning, Phoenix flies away to see where the beetle men are, and he spots them closing in on the ranch and the coast. The Beetle men land and rummage through one building, and Phoenix challenges them. They soon lose two more beetle men as Phoenix burns them to empty husks. Phoenix comes back to warn the women and children to hide and stay quiet. White spot decides he can't lose any more of his army, so he heads them out to sea towards the Island.

Phoenix flies over the water to ensure the beetles are heading to the Island. At the rate they're traveling, it'll take a couple of weeks for them to reach the Island. Phoenix can get to the Island in five days, pushing his strength to the full. Phoenix circles back to the ranch to assure the women they are safe. Phoenix wants permission to stay a few days before he flies to the Island, and it's a trip he's not looking forward to.

Three days later, Phoenix, amid goodbyes and a leather bag full of food they gave to him, Phoenix wished them well and told them to travel to the next village to get help. Phoenix launches into the air and heads out to sea. Phoenix climbs to ten thousand feet to make his trip less harsh at that height; he'd not face any headwinds. It also gives him the vantage point of seeing the beetle men as he catches up to them and flies on by. He sees them floating on the water as he flies high overhead.

Phoenix continues to the Island, and he did manage to fly there for five days nonstop. Arriving before the beetle men, Phoenix collapses in an exhausted state. He lies on the shore for the rest of the day and night. In the morning, he wakes up and is very stiff. Phoenix gets up and walks around to work out the stiffness in his body. The next thing is to break his fast with the food the women gave him before he left New-Land.

Phoenix decides sleeping on the beach is not a good thing, so he flies to the castle to search for a place to stay. His first pick is the blacksmith's shop. With the forge there, he can keep warm. Phoenix then checks out the rest of the Island looking for the portal, and he can't find it. Phoenix realizes he'll have to wait for the beetle men to arrive and show him where it is.

Phoenix flies up to ten thousand feet to look out over to the east of the Island to see if he can detect the beetle men. Phoenix fails to see them. Each day Phoenix flies up to the ten thousand feet to look for the beetle men until they reach the Island. Phoenix does this every day for a week, and one morning he spots a brown smug on the horizon, and he realizes they'll be at the Island in a few days. To keep hidden, Phoenix uses his sparrow form to keep an eye on the beetle men as they land on the Island.

The beetle men land on the shore and seem to drop to the ground; they're exhausted from the flight. For hours Phoenix perches in a nearby tree just watching the beetle men. None of them move until the following morning when the sunrise warms them up, and then they fly to the middle of the Island. Then Phoenix sees the portal; it looks like heat waves on a sweltering day. The beetle men enter the portal and disappear; they do this one at a time, leaving white spot to the last.

White spot stops and scans the area with his antenna. He seems to spot Phoenix in the tree above him, which gives white spot pause, then in a flash, he flies into the portal. Phoenix waits, and then he follows in his sparrow form; he isn't ready for what he sees. The world around him is dead, and at the far end of the valley there are hordes of giant insects of all sizes and types. White spot is waiting for him. And white spot misses slashing Phoenix out of the air as Phoenix enters that world.

Phoenix lands and changes into his human form and draws his sword of starstone. White spot engages Phoenix in a fight. Phoenix keeps dancing out of white spots way and slashes the beetle man on each pass until Phoenix cuts off white spot's antenna, then white spot starts meandering off as if blind and lost. Phoenix leaves white spot, turns to the valley below him, and watches a wave of a thousand insects rushing toward him and the portal. Phoenix sees the two suns, and he draws strength from them, which he used to burn the first wave of insects to ash as they charge up the valley towards him.

This gave the insects pause, and then the second wave started moving up the valley to the portal. Phoenix burns the second wave of insects. This makes the third wave hold back. Phoenix realizes that he can't keep this up they'll eventually overwhelm him and re-enter his world.

Phoenix is watching the insect armies to see what they will do next. Phoenix doesn't see the hive instructor as she appears next to him and places a hand on his shoulder, nearly frightening him; Phoenix thought he was alone where he stood.

"Phoenix, you have to stop them from reaching the portal, or your world will become like this." Intoned the instructor.

"Thanks a lot for that tidbit of information. It's a bit obvious. If you have a solution to that problem, please share it with me!"

"See that rock spire?" points the instructor.

"Yes, what about it?"

"Melt the base, and it'll fall on top of the portal blocking access to the portal to your world."

Phoenix looks at the spire, "That will take a lot of power; what will keep the insects at bay long enough for me to bring it down?" questions Phoenix.

"You can do it, and I'll watch the insects and warn you if they get too close."

"If you say so!" Phoenix concentrates his heat at the base of the pillar. What helps is that this world has two sons, and he can tap into them to gather more heat to pour into the bottom of the spire. The rock spire is at least half a mile in diameter, so it will take a lot of heat to make the rock molten enough to topple the spire. Phoenix is concentrating so hard on the spire that he doesn't see the insects slowly moving up the valley towards him.

The rock spire's base is red hot; then it becomes yellow hot, then white hot, and turns liquid as lava. All the time he is concentrating on the spire, the top starts to topple in his direction, and it's falling very fast. The insects move more quickly toward Phoenix when the hive instructor grabs Phoenix and pitches him into the portal as the rock spire falls on to the portal blocking it. Not to mention the insects crushed by the spire as it falls on top of the portal. Blocking the insects forever from leaving this world they consumed.

Over time the insects turn on each other and cannibalize one another into extinction. Phoenix realizes the instructor saved his life by pitching him through the portal before the spire fell and blocked the portal. Phoenix becomes concerned that the portal is still visible from this side, so Phoenix decides to block the portal from this side to make sure that no one or thing can use it.

CHAPTER

25

Over the next month, Phoenix removes the castle's stone walls and stacks them up around and on top of the portal; when he finishes stacking the blocks, it's a hundred feet high, a hundred feet wide. Phoenix flies above the construct in the last act, pours all the heat he can pull together, and fuses the stone blocks into one solid block, forever blocking the portal from this side. This took a lot of energy out of Phoenix, and so he spent a few days recovering from his labor.

Phoenix is exhausted and he spent several more days recovering his strength. While Phoenix was resting, he tried to decide which way he would return home. He could spend a couple of months flying west and crossing the land of Randl, or he could fly five days to the east. He is too weary of thinking about it for the time being. Phoenix misses Becky, and so that decides which way he'd go. The five days of flying would bring him home to her faster than the months it would take by going west.

In a week, Phoenix builds up his strength in preparation for the long continuous flight back home. That evening Phoenix eats a big meal and takes a long drink of water. At dawn, he will set out for home. Phoenix launches into the air at dawn and then aims at the sunrise. Phoenix keeps the sun in front, above him, and behind him. At night he follows the stars. At the end of the fifth day, Phoenix spots the west coast of New-Land, and as luck would have it, Phoenix lands next to one of the watches towers he had set up years ago.

The watchtower was occupied by two people keeping an eye on the coast, and they saw Phoenix as he flew in and landed. They were ready to do battle or spread the word of danger by lighting the signal fires. Upon landing, Phoenix collapses into a heap at the base of the tower. One of the watcher's ventures down to see who this person is. They investigate and still didn't know who this person was. They take pity, then covered him up with a blanket, and built a small campfire. In the morning, they wake him up and feed him.

They go out of their way to help this stranger for a few days to let him build back his strength. They take Phoenix into the tower to question him when they discover he's, their king. Phoenix regaled them of what had happened and why he was gone as a reward. They were amazed at his story. They would remember that their king took the time to tell them his story.

The next day Phoenix flies on toward castle Phoenix. Phoenix bypasses the communication center and flies on toward home and Becky. It took Phoenix a few more days to reach the castle, and he lands in the yard of the scribe where Becky is staying. As Phoenix lands, he's not surprised to see Becky waiting for him. Phoenix takes Becky and gives her a greeting as if they had not seen each other in years. Becky became red in the face after the hugs and kisses she receives.

The scribe had stepped out to see the reunion of Phoenix and Becky. He decides to go to the castle to stay the night with his friend, leaving Phoenix and Becky alone at his house. In the morning, the scribe returns with his girlfriend so she can meet the Phoenix. That whole day was spent with the Phoenix retelling his story about stopping the insects from entering their world from Becky's dead world. With a few questions asked by Becky about her home world and the questions asked by the scribes to clarify a few points of Phoenix's story. Phoenix gave the scribes a lot to write about and file in the history library.

The scribes returned to the castle leaving Phoenix and Becky to use the cottage one more night. In the morning, Phoenix and Becky leave to return to their cottage where Phoenix's grandfather lived. Phoenix had returned to using his name as Todd. Phoenix wanted to fade from the limelight, become a legend, and eventually become a myth. To make that happen, he decides to return to where he and Alana once lived down in the valley.

Phoenix takes Becky down into the valley to see the house he built three thousand years ago. It was pretty run down and would need to be taken down to the foundation and rebuilt. When Becky saw it and saw how remote it was, she fell in love with the location. It would mean no one would come and visit them. Becky loved the idea of being alone with her love. Besides, Phoenix can fly them anywhere if they get an itch to see people.

Phoenix removes the rubble and the vegetation; then, he rebuilds the house, the barn, and the smokehouse. Then Phoenix decides to build a new smithy where he can work at being a blacksmith. Phoenix liked working as a blacksmith. He built the smithy and a new forge. Then he moved all their stuff down from his grandfather's cottage, including all the blacksmith tools and supplies.

With the beetle's men's attack starstone became as precious as gold. Phoenix discovers that the valley is full of the starstone, so Phoenix collects it and keeps some of it to work with. On occasion, Phoenix would take a bag full of starstone, and Becky then fly to the outskirts of the new city on the ocean and sell the starstone to brokers who were clamoring to get their hands on them. Todd would earn enough funds to buy Becky some nice things or be able to spend a few days staying in the city. The best thing is knowing that no one knows who they are.

Over the passing years, Phoenix and Becky became unknown to everyone. Phoenix, known as Todd, can travel the world, and no one knows who they are. This allows Phoenix to oversee his kingdoms without being known. Phoenix soon discovers he is no longer needed as the king; the people keep the rulers in check. In a few places where a ruler gets out of hand, he is forceable removed from power and a new ruler put into place by the people.

Over the years, Phoenix gathers many of his tears in small vials; he finds an exciting way to drop them off at the medical school.

Phoenix would fly to castle Phoenix, and in a small bag, Todd and Becky would stay at a nearby inn. Then during the late evening at dusk, Phoenix would fly in his eagle form with the bag to the school. Phoenix would fly in the open the door to the blacksmith shop, drop the bag of tears off next to the greenhouse, change to a sparrow, and fly back out the door. Once Phoenix flew over the castle wall, he would change into an owl to return to the Inn where Becky waited for him.

This kept the legend of Phoenix somewhat alive. Over the years, the legend has become a myth. This suits Phoenix and Becky very well. They've been enjoying not being part of the government. Not a ruler. Just an average unknown couple. Phoenix tried his best to full fill Becky's needs. The one thing that she couldn't have in this world was a child. That hurt her more than she would let on. Phoenix knew this was a sore spot with her; he remembered Alana and how she had a similar problem until they found a homeless baby who they raised as their daughter.

On one of their trips to Castle Phoenix, Todd and Becky land in a secluded wooded area so they wouldn't be seen. Then they'd hike to the castle city. On one such occasion, they hear a baby crying. Becky stops and goes to investigate the cry, followed closely by Todd. They discover a newborn child lying under a tree. Someone had left the child there to die. She was missing all the toes on her left foot, but she looked normal otherwise. Becky picks up the child, and with pleading eyes, she looks at Todd. He smiled as he said yes.

It may not be her child by birth, but it'll be her child to love and care for. The child is hungry. With its crying they head to the Inn where they can get some milk to feed the child. That child couldn't have been loved anymore if Becky had been her actual mother. Todd remembers Raven, his adopted daughter, three thousand years ago and how Alana saved the girl and fought furiously to protect her from the sea raiders just as if Raven were her natural child.

At the Inn and the child was fed and changed into clean clothes. "Well, Becky, are you ready to take care of her until her name day." "What do you mean?" she asks.

"I was wondering. Becky here on this world we call a child kid or girl until they become the age of thirteen when the child picks her name," says Phoenix.

"That seems strange," questions Becky.

"In time, you'll understand; also, at thirteen, she'll be able to change her shape into whatever animals her parents can change into."

"Ok, we'll follow tradition. However, I'll give her a nickname until she picks her name. I'll call her princess."

Todd chuckles; he's happy for Becky. She can now be a mother. For that, he's grateful.

Phoenix and Becky raise the little girl until she has her name day. She grew into a tall maiden with deep brown hair and the most prominent brown eyes. Rebecka was perfect in every way except for her left foot. The missing toes weren't a problem for Rebecka. Phoenix and Becky teach Rebecka all they can. Like how to dance and how to dance with the sword, Math and reading. On her name day, she chooses Rebecka as her name. Rebecka was soon ready to be married, and they took her to the country of Randal to live until she found a young man she would like to marry. A few years after she has married, Rebecka becomes a mother and has several children; Becky enjoys being a grandmother. Becky enjoys getting with them so she can watch over her grandchildren. Soon Phoenix and Becky returned to New-Land to hide that they don't age like others around them. Phoenix and Becky leave the grandchildren, but they would come by and view them from a distance from time to time. And watch them grow and have families.

CHAPTER

26

Over time Phoenix and Becky watches the world as it changes, going from an agricultural world to an industrial one. They also witnessed that over the years, the human side of the people has taken over, and people can't become animals hardly anymore. Some few can change, but over time even they'll lose the animal side of the Chimerians. It has to do with the fact that the Chimerians had to mate as humans and not as animals. This gradual change and the loss of their animal side forced the Chimerians into embracing progress. They can no longer change into animal form and travel as fast as possible. Now they have to rely on other methods of travel.

Steam became the preferred method of traveling the world. They build roads and railroads. They even discovered the telegraph and could send messages anywhere within the country in mere minutes rather than weeks. Sailing ships gave way to steam-powered ships. So instead of several months to cross the oceans, it can be done in a few weeks. Phoenix and Becky have difficulty hiding that they live indefinitely while everyone lives only three hundred years. By this time, Phoenix has died and been reborn so many times that he can't even count the years. Becky is still young-looking, as if she has never aged.

War became unlikely to happen. Phoenix is watching for it in hopes that prosperity will override greed. Cities and towns soon spring up all over both countries. Phoenix can't recognize the world he was born in. Phoenix realizes he has succeeded in his desire to end slavery and war. Over time Todd and Becky change with the world. They became educated to the world's standards and taught history in the collages. By this time, Phoenix had died and been raised from the ashes over ten times, and each time he is reborn, his appearance has undergone some changes, so no one realizes who he was.

Suppose you saw Phoenix when he was reborn this last time. He shined with red and violet color fringed with green fire. And his new human body looked similar as always, just younger. The world moves on with new inventions and problems. In Todd's history class, one of the students asked, "Professor Todd, did the Phoenix ever really exist?"

"You asked the question, what makes you think he didn't exist?" posed Todd.

"If he existed, then where is he? According to the myth of the Phoenix, he's supposed to exist forever, rising from the ashes."

"What you say is true; he should still be alive; what makes you think he's not still around?" asks Todd.

"If he's alive, why has no one seen him?"

"Question, how many of you can change into an alternate form?" asks Todd.

Only a few students raise their hands; Todd changes into an eagle before their eyes.

"As you can see, I'm still a true Chimerian; in the next few generations, those who are true Chimerians will be bred out to be human. Then true Chimerians will become myths over time."

"What does that have to do with the Phoenix? Prof."

"Consider this, what if the Phoenix is real, and all the myths are true about him. But he is no longer needed. What do you think he might do?" queried Todd to his class.

"So, you believe he's alive and well, Prof?"

"Unless you have a compelling argument that he doesn't, I believe he is alive. For all we know, he could be your next-door neighbor. This leads us to your homework for this weekend. I want you to go to the library and research this Phoenix. Answer the question if he existed and if he could be alive today," commands Todd.

"Ah, Prof, this weekend?" moaned a student.

"Yes, and I want ten pages and references for where you got the information," says Todd.

The class is not too happy about the assignment, but Todd almost laughs out loud after the class leaves. Thought to himself, "Or he might be your history teacher."

That night Todd drives by the library to pick up Becky, his wife, in their steam-powered car. Todd drives them to their home just off-campus.

"How did your day go, Becky?" queries Todd.

"Much the same, except that many of your students wanted what they could get on the Phoenix. I assume you were the cause of that?" Becky asked with a raised eyebrow and a smile.

"In a way, it was asked of me if the Phoenix was still alive. I gave them the assignment to pose the question and answer it," smirked Todd.

"I suppose you laughed about that?" stated Becky.

"I did," said Todd.

"Now you've had your fun. Are we going to the big game tonight?" asked Becky.

"Sure, why not? It'll show that we support our university," said Todd.

They went to the exhibition game, something like rugby, to watch and cheer the players on. Toward the end of the game, one of the students is badly injured. And he is carried off the field on a stretcher. In the ambulance, the driver commented that the boy would never walk again. It pretty much was the exact prognoses the doctors had. Becky found out about it and went to Todd to tell him and ask if he would see the boy.

Todd went to see the boy that day, and he took a vial of his tears with him. When Todd got to the boy's room, the doctor was leaving to tell the boy's parents the bad news that he would be paralyzed for the rest of his life. Todd enters the room, and a nurse tells him that he should leave; the only one who can be in here is the boy's family. Todd steps out of the room. Todd waits for the nurse to come out; as the door opens, Todd flies into the room in his sparrow form, Todd drops down to the floor and hops under the boy's bed.

The door closes, and Todd takes his human form. Todd looks around and sees the boy is out, and he would not remember Todd being there. Todd takes out the vial and pours it on the boy's head. "May you heal," whispers Todd, then he leaves the room.

The next day the news was exciting. The boy recovers fully and can walk the next day. The doctor is mystified. All he can say is, "it's not possible!" Todd and Becky chuckle about it. "That felt good," said Todd. "It has been a long-time since I've done anything like that."

Becky takes Todd into her arms to thank him for doing what he did to save that boy.

Chapter

27

Not long after Todd saved the boy, scientists discover a disturbing problem coming their way from space. A giant solar flare is headed there way, and it will kill many people from radiation when it hits the planet. The government is informed, and it's decided not to tell the population what will happen. Why cause a planet-wide panic over something they can't stop.

Todd asks for the homework they were supposed to turn in before he starts today's lesson in class. The student who asked the questions about the Phoenix myth had more questions. "Prof, is not your wife's name Becky?"

"It is; what has that to do with the lesson?" queries Todd.

"Is not your name Todd?"

"Yes, again, what has this to do with the assignment?"

"Prof, in my research, I discovered that Phoenix's wife's name is Becky, and the name the Phoenix used from time to time is Todd, his father's name…"

Some of the students collapsed to the floor in the class, and they were dead. Todd and the other students check them only to find them dead. "Class dismissed; go check your loved ones." Todd dashed out of the class, changing to a falcon, and flew home to check on Becky. Todd enters the front door of his house and calls out her name. Todd doesn't find her until he looks in the backyard. Todd finds her lying on the ground, and she is dead. His tears wouldn't work to save her. She was already dead.

Todd held her and cried; what caused this, he begged and wondered if he would also die, or rather he hoped he would. Phoenix burns Becky's body to ash. He didn't want the world to find out she was an alien. Then on the radio, he heard what was happening. A solar storm will hit this planet, and everyone on it will die. What killed the people in mass was the radiation burst that the flare was putting out. Phoenix didn't care. He lost everything at that moment, but in his heart, he hears Becky and Alana say you must save them if you can. Phoenix pulls himself together and steps into the front yard of his house, changes into the Phoenix, launches into the air and shouts out in a thunderous screech that he is not a myth. Phoenix flies straight up into the air toward the solar flare, and he passes beyond the envelope of air. Phoenix usually flies in and Phoenix sails up to the edge of space to greet the solar flare, which seems timed to meet him as he reaches the edge of the atmosphere.

Phoenix touches and absorbs the solar flare and falls back to earth like a meteor; he is burned up due to the friction as he falls through the atmosphere. Phoenix hits the ground in his phoenix form, causing a crater shaped like a giant phoenix bird. In the crater's center is a massive pile of ash. The crater is on the university campus. Security shows up and ropes off the area. Then security discovers high levels of radiation. They want to keep all the students, teachers, and reporters away for their own protection.

The next day the scientists show up to begin to take readings and samples of the area to determine how to clean it up and make the area safe. The second day passes without incident just more tests and security keep the curious away from the crater for their own protection. One of the students climbs one of the towers on campus to take a picture of the crater. Later that picture would become famous.

On the third day, things happened that no one could explain until a student from Todd's history class put the pieces together. Phoenix explodes out of the ashes and stands there in his human form, all golden, and a bright light shined from him, covering up that he was naked. Then he looks up and explodes like a pheasant exploding from under a bush into the air. Scaring everyone as he launches into the air, Phoenix thunders out in a screech as he disappears straight into the sky.

Phoenix was being watched as he headed for space, and they watch him as he leaves the planet, never to return. The world didn't need him anymore, and so Phoenix decides to go someplace away from planet Randle and the Chimerians. Is this the end? Maybe.

Epilog

As the student from Professor Todd's class who asked the question about the Phoenix, I managed to put some clues together. I'm sure that the Phoenix was Todd, and Becky, his wife, is the long-lived wife of old. Professor Todd's phrasing of his questions about the Phoenix still being around and living among us made me suspicious. I dug into the subject over the weekend and discovered the myth of the Phoenix and how he was reborn in fire and ash. Then I found that his tears could heal, and I recalled the rugby player. The doctor said he would never walk again. And then a miracle happened, and none of the doctors could explain it.

There was a funny thing about Professor Todd and his wife. He didn't exist in any of our records until a hundred years ago—no records of birth or where they lived. The Phoenix just appeared here on campus and saved the world one last time; then he flew off. I decided to go to the professor's house to see him. The front door was open when I got there, and no one is around. I check the backyard, and I don't see any one; I did see some fine ash in the form of a person. I looked closer and found a necklace and a bracelet shaped like a Phoenix in flight.